# BLACK HELICOPTERS

# BLACK
# HELICOPTERS

BLYTHE WOOLSTON

CANDLEWICK PRESS

*This book was built with courage borrowed from Sarah Davies and Elizabeth Bicknell.*

Copyright © 2013 by Blythe Woolston

First edition 2013

Library of Congress Catalog Card Number 2012942619

ISBN 978-0-7636-6146-5

13 14 15 16 17 18 BVG 10 9 8 7 6 5 4 3 2 1

Printed in Berryville, VA, U.S.A.

This book was typeset in Minion.

Candlewick Press
99 Dover Street
Somerville, Massachusetts 02144

visit us at www.candlewick.com

*To the ones we need to see*

*The mind knows only
what lies near the heart.*
— *Elder Edda*

# LAST NIGHT

I stand rock steady on their hands. It's not that hard really; we've practiced. Neither of them will start drinking until their part is over, and their part is holding me above the heads of the rest of the crowd, above the highest reach of the flames from the bonfire. The men have become my legs, and I'm a twelve-foot-tall, four-legged girl because that's what I need to be. Because that's what they need me to be.

Wolf says, "Tell us, what do you see?"

"I see my mother and my father, waiting for me," I say, but I see nothing like that. I see the chopped path of moonlight on the black lake water. My father, my mother, I do not see. I can't remember my mother's arms. I can't remember my father's eyes. I cannot walk into the past any more than I can walk across the lake on moonlight.

The men lower me until I can rest my hands on their shoulders. They lift me up again when Wolf says, "Tell us, what do you see?"

"I see a green world, and you all are there," I say, but what I really see is how the sparks from the fire rise up when the logs collapse. They float into the sky and disappear. They are only sparks. The stars are only sparks too, I guess. They will blink out some day. They will be swallowed by a ravenous wolf. With each star's passing, the cold and the dark will be more absolute. It will be so cold that snow will not fall. Even the snow will be dead. I've seen the future.

They lower me, and this time, I feel a hand on the inside of my thigh. To steady me? I'm steady. Maybe just to touch me because he can. Then I'm lifted again. Wolf is almost shouting now. "Tell us, what do you see."

"I see Valhalla," I say. "Hel has parted the curtains between the worlds, and I see where she sleeps. She welcomes me."

I see Wolf's face, and he is not happy. I was supposed to see him, not Hel. I see the frame of birch saplings lashed together to be a window to the next world, and I see those silly girls, Stormy and Sky, Wolf's daughters, holding it. They have already lost interest in the ceremony, so the frame is wobbling a little bit. It doesn't matter to them. They don't need to see through it to the other side. This is the present. They lower me to the ground, and then the two men walk me away from the fire, away from the lakeshore, to the place where precious and dangerous things are kept. Precious and dangerous things like me.

The door to the Quonset is locked from the outside. There is one little window; during the day, light sneaks through the wire-reinforced glass and dirt. Now all the light is inside, galvanized and grey, bouncing off the curved walls. It's locked in here with me.

I've got nothing to do until Wolf and Eva show up. I could sit on my cot. I could strip naked and wait under my wool blanket. Both of those things seem like too much trouble. Pretty soon, I'm not going to have any kind of trouble ever again.

Wolf and Eva are at the door. I can hear the keys in the locks. The door amplifies every sound, but that is no surprise to me. I've lived here long enough. The door scrapes open. Wolf is carrying the computer. Eva is carrying my new clothes.

Wolf has rigged a tripod to hold the laptop camera steady. Now he needs to be sure that the picture is framed just right. He drags a box in front of it and then pulls the blanket off the cot and folds it. It will be a comfortable place to sit. The flags hang from a wire behind me. They are hanging flat so they will be easy to see. They are part of the message.

Eva brings the big metal washtub from the corner where I keep it. We had one like it at home. I was so little then, I could curl up under it and hide safe as a turtle. I stand up and pull off my hoodie, my T-shirt. I bend over to unlace my boot, but Eva is kneeling to help me, so I just wait while she loosens the laces. She lifts one foot at a time and pulls my boots off. I'm not rock steady now; I have to reach out and brace myself against her. She takes off my wool socks. Bo taught me I should always keep my socks dry. My socks are dry.

"Can I see Bo?"

"No, honey. You can see him in the morning. You both have other work to do right now," says Eva.

I haven't seen Bo for days. I don't know how many days.

I can hear Stormy and Sky coming up the path. Those two are always noisy as squirrels. They carry white plastic buckets full of hot water for my bath. I need to smell like an ordinary girl tomorrow. I need to wash the wood smoke out of my hair. I step into the tub and Eva uses a coffee can to pour water over my head. Then she squirts soap on my hair. My scalp tingles. I smell like peppermint now, because it is peppermint soap. She washes my hair and my ears.

"Close your eyes, honey," says Eva, so I do. If I get soap

in my eyes, it will make me cry. I need to be clear-eyed. Eva washes my arms from my shoulders to my hands. She washes my breasts and between my legs. Then she washes my legs all the way down to my feet. Then she rinses me, once, twice, three times, and wraps a rough towel around my shoulders.

"She should wait until her hair dries." Eva is talking to Wolf. "Your hair looks so pretty and white." Eva is talking to me.

"We got all night," says Wolf.

"She needs to sleep, too," says Eva. "Go get the food now, girls. Get a move on." Stormy and Sky move slower than usual, if that's possible.

"Well, we can get her dressed and make sure everything is set up right. She can do it after she eats — or whenever," says Wolf.

Eva hands me underpants, and I put them on. She helps me adjust the straps on the bra. I don't usually wear one, but I need to have one on tomorrow. She slides a pale blue T-shirt over my head. Eva picked it out to match my eyes. She hands me some jeans. The denim is new and dark. Then she leads me to the box and I sit down.

"Do you want your shoes on now, honey?" Eva asks.

I usually wear my boots day and night unless I'm wading through water and I need to keep them dry. I don't know if I want to wear these little silver shoes or go barefoot.

I stick out my foot and Eva pushes a shoe into place. It pinches my toes. I shake my head, and Eva takes it off.

"You have to wear them tomorrow," Eva says.

I know what I have to do tomorrow. When the time comes, I'll wear the pinchy silver shoes.

"And this," says Eva, and she drapes a hoodie over the end of the cot. It has a camo pattern, but the colors are turquoise, white, and baby blue. I can't imagine any place where those colors would help a person hide, but Eva says I will blend right in with other people if I wear it. It is part of my disguise.

Stormy and Sky are back. Stormy is carrying a drinking horn and a quart box of milk. Sky has a wooden tray holding a bowl of Honey Nut Cheerios and dishes of smoked salmon, black cherries, and chocolate. These are the things I like to eat.

"Let's get you set up," says Wolf. So I turn to face the computer. He thumbs the clicker, and I can see myself on screen. The flags behind me are bright: red, white, and black; red, white, and blue; yellow, black, and green. The flags are always there. They will be there tomorrow.

"Let's get this on you now," says Wolf, and he wraps my black vest around me. The weight settles on my shoulders. It is a comfort to me. "The detonator isn't rigged. We'll do that in the morning. You can even take it off after you get done recording. I won't rivet up the straps."

Eva steps forward and rubs my hair between her fingers. "Almost dry already!" She brings me the drinking horn. "Just a sip now. You need to be real clear when you tell your story." The mead tastes funny tonight, but every batch is different, because the honey is always different. It depends on the flowers the bees find. I don't know the taste of these flowers, that's all.

"You just go ahead and talk as long as you like. Don't worry about making mistakes. We can edit it down and have it ready by the time you finish your job. So you just go ahead and say whatever you need to say — the battery is charged up and there is plenty of memory," says Wolf.

"Can I have the kerosene lantern?" I ask. I like the yellow light. It doesn't glare as hard as the LEDs. The shadows cast by the live fire are softer. It throws a little heat, too. I shouldn't feel cold — the night isn't cold — but I do. I want the comfort of the kerosene. We used kerosene most nights at home, at least during dinner. When I remember my home, I remember being in that warm light.

"Sure, honey," says Eva. She lights the lamp suspended from the arching metal ceiling. "Anything else you need, you just knock on the door. We'll have a man out there all night. Anything you need."

I stare at the screen. The girl I see there might as well be a picture in a book; she is so still. I never see her blink, because my own eyes close when that happens. I stare at her and it seems we have nothing to do with each other.

I swallow and take a deep breath.

"I'm Valkyrie White. I'm fifteen. Your government killed my family."

# ELEVEN YEARS AGO

We are sitting at the table. I am eating peanut butter and jam. Da is teaching Bo some numbers. We all hear the helicopter. Pock-a-pock-pock-POCK-A-POCK! Pock-pock-pock. It is right over the house where we sit at the table. I am eating peanut butter and jam.

Mabby is outside, in the garden, picking beans. The sun is high, and it is the best time to pick them. I am going to help. I must pick them carefully, each bean. I must not tug and tear the vines. I must leave the tiny beans to grow until the-day-after-tomorrow.

First, I must eat my peanut butter and jam and show Da how I can read: "He, me, be, we," I can read, "my, try, sky, fly."

Now Mabby, the garden, the beans — the tiny beans for the-day-after-tomorrow.

But the-day-after-tomorrow doesn't come.

Mabby is sleeping in the dirt.

Da runs to Mabby in the garden. He turns her face to the sky, but her eyes don't blink. He puts his finger on her throat. He pulls his hand back like Mabby is a stove full of fire. There isn't a mark on her — no blood — no cuts. The beans spill out of the colander. The vines are mashed and broken where she fell. When she wakes up she is going to be angry about the beans.

"Git to the house," Da says. Then he picks up Mabby and carries her to the truck.

When it is dark, Bo makes me drink some milk and go to bed.

In the morning, Da is there, but Mabby isn't. Mabby never again.

When a piece is gone from the game, the whole game changes. That's how it is for us.

Mabby was a really important piece.

We used to eat vegetables from the garden and eggs from the chickens. We used to drink milk from the goats. But the garden, the chickens, the goats — those were Mabby's deal. She took care of all that. She planted and weeded and picked. She fed the chickens and gathered the eggs and butchered the chickens that didn't lay eggs. She milked the goats, morning and evening. Now Mabby's gone, those things don't happen.

Da can't do that stuff, because he has to go to work sometimes.

The goats go first. Da loads them in the back of the truck and they go away. After that, we drink milk out of cans. That milk isn't good. It is gloopy and yellow and smells funny. Da says we have to drink it anyway or our bones will get soft.

Bo and I tried to help with the chickens, but we let them get out. That's OK for a while, but then they wandered away or coyotes stole them. No eggs. Da said that didn't matter. Meat is as good as eggs. Meat makes muscles.

Then the snow comes and covers the garden. We still have jars of food that Mabby made, but when they are emptied, we never filled them up again. Da just throws them out into the place where the garden used to be. Sometimes the jars break. Da says we should never go in Mabby's garden, because we might get hurt on the broken glass.

After a while, we never eat Mabby food anymore. We eat survival food and MREs. Da lets us put ketchup and syrup on it. That makes it better.

· · ·

"Come out here," yells Da.

I wonder what we did wrong. I don't want to get hit. When Da yells, sometimes he hits too. I hope it was Bo, not me. But if Bo did it, I probably did it too.

Da dumps a lump and rag of blood and fur out of a bag. It's a coyote. It was a coyote. Now it's an empty body, a tail, paws pacing without moving. It has teeth, a tongue, and a bullet hole in the gut.

Da picks up the coyote and hangs it over the wide, black post by the gate to our property. "Get me the hammer and a big nail," says Da. We run. Bo carries the hammer. I carry the nail. "Hold this here," Da says to Bo. He means the dead body of the coyote. I hold out the big nail before Da asks.

Da adjusts the coyote so the head is right on top the post and says, "Keep it right there." I step up to help Bo, but I'm careful not to get in the way. I grab the fur on the coyote's shoulder and push it hard against the fence post. I'm doing my part. Da shoves the spike into one of the coyote's eyes. When he brings the hammer down, bone crunches and blood spatters. I turn my head and shut my eyes. I don't want coyote blood in my eyes.

"It's done," says Da. "When you see this, I want you to remember: Those People will kill us like coyotes. We are nothing to them but coyotes."

That is why we must stay in the den when he is away working.

Otherwise, Those People will kill us like coyotes.

"What do you do if black helicopters come?" Da asks.

"Hide," I say.

"Hide where?" Da asks.

"In the den," I say.

"What do you do if you hear a helicopter while you're outside?" Da asks.

"Hide," I say.

"Hide where?" Da asks.

"I hide in mineral," I say.

"Be specific," says Da.

"Under truck, metal roof, cut bank, big rock."

Da falls silent. I know he's thinking about Mabby. He will never forget about Mabby. He reaches out and pets my hair. "Good girl, Valley. Good girl."

The den is a safe place Da made for us under the floor. It is big enough for one bunk. Bo and I have to sleep heads to tails, but we each have our own sleeping bag. I say Bo's feet smell. He says mine do too. Sometimes, we have kickfights, but that isn't fun for very long.

. . .

I am surprised sometimes that Bo isn't me. I'm the girl. He's the boy. I *know* that. Different bodies. I *know* that. *We* know that. We sleep in the same bunk. We know.

Da gives us books and clocks to make the time go faster when he is away. We read the books: fox, socks, box. And the clocks? While he is gone, we use tiny screwdrivers and tweezers to take them apart. Sometimes we work together, four hands on one clock.

"Put this together again," says Da. "See if you can make the pieces fit and make it tick." So then that is what we want to do. We take them apart to see how they tick. We put them together and listen to them tock. Da is very proud of us.

Tick, tick, tick.

Tock, tock, tock.

Bo is Bo. I am me. And together we are we.

We fix clocks. We wear socks. We fix clocks while we wear socks.

# THIS MORNING

We each have our own expertise. Eva's is putting on mascara.

"Look up, honey, don't blink."

I don't flinch.

"I shoulda put this on last night. It really makes your eyes pop. But then you woulda woke up a mascaraccoon. You know what that is, honey?" Eva pauses and licks her finger and moves to scrub a mistake off my skin.

"Sssst!" I say. Eva freezes. I can't believe she was actually going to put her spit on my face.

"Lip gloss?"

I say nothing.

"I'll just put it in your coat pocket. Put some on before," says Eva. "What's this?" She's found a wool sock in my pocket. It is full of chocolate left from last night. My other pocket is full of wool sock and smoked salmon.

"My feet get cold in these shoes," I say. "I can wear the socks in the truck."

Eva opens her mouth to talk about that, but Wolf cuts her off. "Doesn't matter. It's time to leave."

"Where's Bo?" If we need to go, I need Bo now.

"He's sleeping it off, honey. Dolph will be the driver. It's not a problem," says Eva.

"Bo drives. That's the plan."

"The mission is still the same. It's just Dolph will be driving. That's all. It's no big deal."

It kind of is a big deal. Dolph is a mouth-breathing idiot.

"I want to talk to Bo."

"He's still sleeping, honey."

"I want to talk to Bo."

Eva looks at Wolf. Wolf looks at Eva. Wolf tips his head. Eva sighs. "OK, honey. Let's go see. He's at the guys' trailer."

There's a path through the woods from the Quonset to the faded green and white single-wide where the guys sleep. The pine needles are slippery under the little silver shoes. I have to make my steps small and watch where I put my feet. My feet are almost naked, cold and skinny as trout. I shouldn't have to look at them. Stupid shoes, they make me look at my feet like a slave.

. . .

16

Bo is belly down on one of the couches at the front of the trailer. His face is turned to the back. The couch and carpet look wet. If he really was drinking, maybe he spewed. The whole room smells like spilled beer, old puke, and patchouli.

"Bo." He doesn't move. I shake his shoulder. Nothing.

"He had a real lot to drink, honey. He just needs to sleep it off."

I shove his shoulder harder, but all I get is a little noise he makes when he sucks in his breath. He doesn't even reach up and try to swat my hand away. If I could rouse him, he still wouldn't be in shape to drive. He's fucked up the mission. I can't wait for him to get his shit together. I lean over and kiss him on the cheek. His face doesn't smell like puke; it smells like sweat and iron.

"Bye, Bo," I whisper in his ear. There's some dried blood inside, and a dark little track dribbles down by the back of his jawbone. He's not fit to drive. "*Abalu, gree-ah.* Bye, Bo."

## Ten Years Ago

We can play chess.

"This is the queen," says Da. "She can move all of these ways." He slides the piece along the board, back and forth, side-to-side, and corner-to-corner. "She is the most powerful piece on the board."

"This is a pawn. He's kind of a little guy." Da taps the little round head of the piece. "The first time a pawn moves, it gets to take two baby steps, one, two. But mostly they just march along, one step at a time. If another piece is in front of him, he's just stuck. He can fight, but only if the other piece is right close, kitty-corner."

"You aren't reading," says Da. "You are just looking at the pictures."

"I am too reading. I know the words."

"You just got it memorized. That's not reading," says Da.

I look at the pictures. There are mice dressed up in beautiful clothes. They live in a house. When I look at the pictures, I hear the words in my head. It sounds like my Mabby.

"You need some more books. Some books without rabbits with clothes on. Rabbits don't wear clothes, Valley," says Da. Then he walks over to the cook stove and shoves my book in the fire.

"They wasn't rabbits," I say. "They was mice."

"Mice don't wear clothes either," says Da.

In the morning, I sneak and check to see if the book is all burnt up. It is ashes, mostly ashes, but there are some pictures that didn't burn all the way. The edges are black, and the paper is brittle and brown, but I still have a mouse in a blue dress.

I hide the bits of pages in the den.

Bo knows I have them, but he doesn't care.

We are so, so happy to hear his truck tires on the gravel. We don't climb out of the den, but we are so, so happy. Da says we can't trust our ears; that one truck sounds like another; that we should never come out until we hear his voice give the all clear. But our ears know the sound of our own Da, and our bodies are so excited we almost squirm out of our skin.

"Pickled beets." It's Da's voice. It's the all-clear words. Bo and I both hit the ladder at the same time, and we are fighting a little bit to see who gets up first, but it's both of us really since our arms and legs are so tangled up together.

"Did I say pickled beets?"

We nod. We are sure he did. We heard it. I'm maybe a little afraid I made a mistake, but no, Da's face is happy. We got it right.

"I should have said cherries." Da points at the table. There's a whole big flat box of dark cherries.

"The job was up at the big lake," says Da. "And I thought about how much my pups love cherries."

We do love cherries, but we never had so many before. Who knew there were so many cherries in the whole world? Da carries the box out onto the back porch. The summer heat smells like pine needles. The summer heat tastes like cherries, black as blood blisters, but juicy and sweet.

Bo and I sit on the porch with the box of cherries between us and crush them into our mouths so fast the juice runs down to our elbows. We spit the seeds like target practice. Then we spit at each other — not just the seeds but chewed-up cherry juice jam. It spatters us both. Then we rest. We stretch out on the porch boards and slowly, slowly eat cherries while the big white clouds scoot across the blue glass sky.

I'm the first one who has to run to the outhouse. My insides are full of growling cherries, fighting and biting to get out. The door bangs open. It's Bo. The cherries are eating him, too. Then I don't do anything except hunch over and hang on until I am just a shaking skin full of nothing at all. I'm afraid to stand up and pull up my pants. I'm afraid the cherries aren't done with me yet. So I just sit there on one hole and Bo sits on the other while the shiny, droning flies bang against the screen on the outhouse window. They sound like cherry pits spit out so hard they buzz before they hit.

After a while, Da calls us. He strips our clothes off and stands us side by side on the rock by the front door. Then he pours buckets of water over us and washes us off from our head to our feet.

"Maybe you know now," he said. "About cherries. Do you want some more?"

"Yes." I did. I think Bo did too, but he didn't say it.

Da laughs and says, "There's a few for tomorrow. Maybe don't eat them so fast. Now, though, you are going to bed. But one thing more. I got you some new books. I want you to try hard and learn the words, not just look at the pictures."

There are no animals with clothes on in the book Da

puts in my hands. It is just a thin little book, but there are many pictures on each page. Da points to a girl with wings on her hat. "See her, Valley? She is a valkyrie."

I take the book and look at the pictures. The valkyrie has a knife and a horse. It's a pretty good book, I decide. I don't think I'll miss my mouse and her blue dress.

"Look," says Da, and he points to a word on the cover. The letters are squiggly, but when Da says, "It says raven," I know it is true.

The long daylight of summer isn't over, but it feels good to climb under the covers in my loft bed, naked and clean. I think I'm going to read until it's too dark, and that would be hours and hours, but I fall asleep before the sun does.


The words in my new book are difficult. The pictures help me know the story. This is a great battle. Here the father is dying. Now the valkyries ride out of the sky, and they are beautiful. These others, green with pointed teeth, they should not be trusted. It is interesting, but confusing. I think maybe I will need Da to read it to me one time, to help me learn, but then I turn the page and there is an animal with clothes on. It isn't a rabbit, but that won't make any difference to Da. He will burn this book if he sees it, I think, so I keep it hidden in the den.

Every day, I study my book. Some words I know: PICKLE, QUEEN, BRAVE. Some words Bo helps me know. He can read better than me because Mabby taught him. Mabby would have taught me, too, but Mabby is gone. Bo likes my book, so he doesn't mind.

Some words do their own talking: the sword swings, "SKRAATH," and the storm shrieks, "HAAOOOOOWL." I copy the words I don't know carefully, exactly as the letters are in the book: AVALANCHE, ABYSS, CHAOS. When I show that list to Da, he says that is smart, to work hard that way. He pets my hair away from my eyes and touches me on the nose. He teaches me each word, how to say it and what it means. Then I have to take the words back with me and see how they work in the story.

Bo and I have a long talk about some of the words in my book. The letters, if they are letters, do not look right. Are they letters? Are they words? It seems to be the things that ravens are saying.

We stand on the porch and see if we can talk to ravens. We try to sound like they do, but we don't know what we are saying. Whatever we are saying does not seem to be very interesting, because the birds hardly ever talk back. When the ravens do answer, they might be telling us to shut up. We don't know. We try using the names for ravens we learned in the book. "Hugin! Munin!" we yell in people talk, but the ravens don't pay any attention to that either.

. . .

There is a dead raven in the woods. We think, at first, somebody shot it. Maybe Those People don't like ravens. Maybe they kill them like coyotes. But when we turn it over and look, there isn't any bullet hole. There is just a dead raven. Its claws are drawn up into bony little fists.

Bo takes off his knife and cuts off one foot and drops it in his pocket.

"Feel this, Valley," he says while he pets the raven. Under my fingers, the feathers are like soft glass, shiny as a black mirror.

"I'm going to take these for you, Valley." Bo is sliding the point of his knife into the joint where a wing meets the body. He takes off both wings, very neatly. Bo is good with a knife. He is a good butcher.

"I'm going to put these on your hat. Valkyries have wings on their hats," says Bo. Bo is a good brother.

Mites and maggots are hatching in my wool hat.

"They came out of the feathers. They came for the raven," says Da. "We should burn it up, and get a new hat."

I don't want to give up my beautiful hat. "Maybe we can just bake it in the oven for some days?" I bargain.

"Well, we can try that way," says Da, "but I get to look at it before you wear it again. I don't want mites and maggots living on you. And you kids should maybe not play with dead things when you find them. It's different than if you kill it. You don't know how it died. It might be poison, or it might be sickness. A person doesn't know, so a person shouldn't play with dead things."

We put my valkyrie hat in the oven. The maggots stop moving and the mites stop crawling. I have to shake the dead ones out very gently so I don't mess up the wings.

The wings aren't spread out like in the pictures of the valkyries; they are closed and drooping down. They are heavy for the hat, but I don't mind. When I run, or when the wind blows hard, sometimes the wings lift up and I imagine they spread out like a flying bird. That's good enough for me.

"It is time to learn more chess pieces," says Da. "This one, the horse one, is called a knight. He's a tricky one. He can jump over other ones."

"That's what a horse is good for, jumping."

"Yes, but that's not all of it. He doesn't go straight. He always goes a little bit sideways too." Da moves the horse in the funny L-shaped paths it can travel.

"The valkyries in my book ride horses. They are kind of like knights."

"Well, yes, they kind of are."

"Will we have horses one day?"

"I hope it doesn't come to that. We got a truck. A truck is better. I think all the valkyries got trucks now, too. But they still wear the hats with the feathers on. . . ." When I look at Da's face instead of the knight in his fingers, I see he's teasing now. He's got a little-boy smile playing hide-and-seek under his whiskers.

"Da!"

"Let's get serious now. Let's see how fast you can learn. You show me where this knight can go."

No fire, don't go outside in the daytime, and no flashlights anywhere except the den. Those are the rules. As long as we follow the rules, the black helicopters can't get us. He knows he can trust us. If he ever finds out different, then he'll have to lock us inside. Nobody wants that. Da says it's good we don't like being trapped. He says it means we are free people. He says he knows it is confusing. For now, we have to be cooped up a little, like chickens. We know what happened when the chickens had their freedom. The world is a bad place, and too much freedom was bad for chickens. It is bad for children too.

# THIS MORNING

I can't lean back into the seat of the U-Haul truck because my vest gets in the way. So I perch forward and stare out the window. Nothing I see matters. The big rolls of hay, the trailers surrounded by junk and clunkers, the hillsides where all the trees are burnt to black bristles. I just look at those things because they are there when I open my eyes.

"Gas," says Dolph, but then he pulls right past the pumps and parks between a big silver tanker truck and a sky-scraping sign that says THE BEAVER TRAP—BEST TAILS IN THE WEST. At night the neon beaver's tail probably flashes up and down, but it's not night and stopping for this is ridiculous. Live Nude Exotic Dancers are not part of the mission.

"Gimme forty-five minutes," says Dolph.

We've already had the conversation about time and the plan. Dolph says he can make up time — there's no reason to drive so slow on the open interstate. He's wrong. We can't call attention to the truck, and we might if we go too fast. Bo understood those things. Bo *taught* me those things. But it is impossible to teach Dolph anything. Dolph is a waste of skin. His brain is made of earwax. His mom should have flushed the toilet on his birthday.

I wish I could kill him right here, but I need him to drive.

Two ravens swoop in front of the windshield and glide to land on the posts of a ragged barbwire fence at the far end of the parking lot. They are big and still and looking right at me. I jerk the door handle up and jump down onto the asphalt. The ravens are waiting for me, so I walk across the lot, past the Beaver Trap, past the casino, past a restaurant, until I come to the edge of the field.

There is a dry irrigation ditch between the fence and me where the two birds sit on top of the wooden posts. The sunlight on their feathers turns black to silver. They are shiny and bright-edged as volcanic glass. They are obviously magic. Odin's ravens: Hugin and Munin, Thought and Memory. I'm not sure which is which.

I slide down the bank of the ditch and hunker at the bottom, looking up at the ravens. One looks at me. The other rustles its wings like a fan.

"I'm here," I say.

The sound of the explosion is loud enough to knock me onto my knees, even though the bank of the ditch protects me. The weight of my vest pulls me forward until I'm flat on the ground before the second explosion moves over me in a stink of heat.

When I open my eyes, the ravens are gone, turned into black smoke that chokes the sun into a little silver spot. My ears aren't right. I crawl along the bottom of the ditch away from that place. I crawl and crawl until I come to some cottonwood trees. Then I let myself climb to the top of the ditch bank and look back.

Stupid Dolph wasted the truck bomb on some scumbags and strippers and waitresses with tired feet. Stupid, stupid Dolph. This is not according to plan.

I hear a siren. My ears are recovering. They still feel full of water, but I hear the siren. It is coming from the blacktop road that connects the town, whatever town it is, to the interstate. It is a little red fire truck. Good luck, little truck. Maybe you can keep the fire from spreading into the empty fields or up the hill to the on-ramp. I hear other sirens now — troopers probably. Guys with fast cars and guns are more useless than that little red truck, but they are coming anyway. Those People will be on the scene.

I could walk up to the volunteer firefighters and the troopers and blow them up. I might even kill some paramedics. It's an opportunity, but not much of one. It is only marginally less wasteful than standing in the middle of the field and using the vest to flip some dirt and dried-up cow patties into the air. I can do better.

If I want to do better, I can't hang around here. The question is, Where should I be instead? And how am I going to get there? Hitching a ride is easier on the two lanes than the interstate. Bo taught me that. He also taught me that hitching is the last resort. Hitching means giving up control. Giving up control is always the last resort. But the highway between the town and the place where the Beaver Trap used to be is too exposed. It will be the site of abnormal activity. People will be noticing things, and I don't want to be noticed.

I climb up onto the ditch bank. There is a path, not much used. It is dotted with scrub willow here and there, so there is some cover. Not that anyone will be looking at the ditch banks. A ditch bank is far less interesting than the fire and the smoke and the flashing lights, glittering blue and red. It isn't a direct path into town, but it is the way to go. Here in the fields, no eye will see me because no eye will look. I'm as invisible as a cow or a bale of hay.

# Eight Years Ago

It is time for us to learn about work.

"It is always best to buy used stuff," says Da. "And don't buy it close to home." Then he pushes the glass door open, a little bell rings, and we go in. Bo and I are holding hands. We must not let go of each other, and we must not touch anything in the store. We may look, but no touching.

It is a very big place. There are so many clothes. We follow Da between clothes and clothes and clothes. The air tastes funny. I pull my sleeve over my nose so I don't have to smell when I breathe.

"We need to get our Valley a dress," says Da, and he stops in front of a wall of colors, dresses in so many sizes. Da unhooks one hanger from the rest and holds the limp yellow dress in front of me. "Too big." Another one, red and

31

white with cherries — I like cherries — but Da says, "Too little." Then a pink one with little flowers made of ribbons. "Just right. You keep ahold of this." He wraps the dress around the hanger and puts it in my hand.

Then Da leads us on, out of the canyons of clothes to a wall full of books.

"Bo, you get to pick a new book."

Bo points to a book with a shiny green cover and red words. He doesn't touch it. He waits for Da to touch it. Da picks it up and reads, *"Tarzan of the Apes."* He opens it and looks at the pages. "You sure this is the one you want? There are some big words in here: carcass, barbaric ornaments, dexterity. This isn't an easy book."

Bo just nods. Yes, this is the book he wants.

Da puts the book in his hand. Bo can see it close now and so can I. There's a guy wearing underpants and a knife. He has a monkey. I want this book too. Bo made a good decision. I like that book way more than I like this stupid dress.

Then we walk on past glass bluebirds and cups and things-I-don't-know-what-they-are. Da picks a clock up from the shelf; he turns it over and looks inside. "Batteries," he says. "All the clocks got batteries now. Got to go to a damn antique store to get a decent windup." He puts the clock back on the shelf and leads us back toward the door.

There is a woman waiting at the counter.

Da says, "Put the stuff up here."

She picks it up and smiles. "Did you find everything you needed?"

Da nods and gives her money. I know Da would have liked a different kind of clock. I know I would have liked a different kind of dress.

"Your children have such good manners," says the woman. "Can I give them a little present?"

"Yes," says Da. "They are good kids."

The woman hands me a plastic woman no bigger than a hammer handle. "You can make her some clothes." The plastic woman is totally naked. Her hair — she has a lot hair — is a fuzzy yellow clump.

"This is for you," she says to Bo. "Oh, I'm sorry. . . . Do you let him play with guns? I know some folks now they don't want their kids playing with toy guns."

"Not a problem," says Da. Then the woman smiles and puts the gun into Bo's hand.

"You all come back again," says the woman, then she turns to the next customer, who has an armful of clothes she wants to buy. She is carrying more clothes than we got in our whole family.

We learn how to use light switches and flush the toilet at the motel. We learn about TV there too. TV is like a window. Push the button: see another window, but sometimes the window changes even if you don't push the button. A shark is banging against a cage, trying to eat the man inside. That's interesting, but then the window changes.

"I want the shark!" I slap the TV with my hand.

"Stop that!" says Da. "TV isn't like books. It has commercials. Wait a minute and the shark and the man will be back. See, there it is."

And the shark *is* back, and it's biting the bars of the cage just like before, but the story doesn't get more interesting. The shark never gets the man. And the commercials keep interrupting it at the good parts. I don't like TV much.

Bo has his new book, and I try to peek at the story, but he can read faster than me and he turns the page before I'm ready. I pick up a book I found when I was looking in the drawers. The drawers were all empty, except for that one book.

"No, Valley," says Da. "Not that one. That book's all full of what you oughta do and what you can't do. It's not a book for free people, Valley. A motel nightstand book is not for us. You shoulda brought your own book. You do that next time."

I don't feel very much like a free people. I'm not supposed to play with the light switches. I'm not supposed to duck under the curtains and look out. I can't make the TV do what I want. I'm in a room that smells like other people with a book I shouldn't read. I don't feel free, not one bit at all.

We are at a playground. Bo's mission is to go and play. My mission is to need Da.

He hardly looks like my Da. He shaved off his whiskers. That is part of the mission, too.

Da puts me on the swing and gives me an underdog push. I am high up in the sky. I wish I had my valkyrie hat, but Da says that's for home. Here, on the playground, I need to wear this pink dress that flutters. The valkyries wear dresses, I think, but not like this one. Da says never mind about what valkyries wear; little girls wear this kind of clothes, and I need you to be a little girl on this mission.

Then it's time for us to eat lunch. We sit on the bench and Da gives us food to eat from a paper bag. We have practiced eating this food before. I think it is good. Bo thinks the green food is disgusting, so Da has to say, "No lettuce. No pickle."

Da points to a woman on a bench. She is talking to another woman. They call to their children: "Be careful! Come here! That's great!"

Da says, "Watch her. See what she does."

She calls to her children, "Time to go!"

She walks across the playground to them. They aren't

listening to her. She picks up an empty bottle. She picks up a paper bag. "Come on! Time to go! I'm going home!" She puts the garbage in a trash can.

"What do you see?" asks Da.

"A woman. She is going home," says Bo.

"She picks things up," I say.

"Yes! That's it, Valley! You saw it," says Da. "That lady is a judge. My customers are angry with her because she legislates from the bench. They want to send her a message, but she doesn't open unexpected mail anymore. But we know how to make sure she gets the message, don't we, Valley? We know how to put it into her hands."

I'm not sure I do understand, but I pretend I do. "Bo, you should eat lettuce. Then your eyes would work better," I say.

"Be nice, Valley!" says Da. "We all have our expertise. Bo will help me build the message for the lady. Bo is very good with his hands. You are good with your eyes, Valley. You notice how people are. Both are good. Together, great."

# Eight Years Ago

## BOMB INJURES CIRCUIT JUDGE

A judge was severely injured Thursday morning when a bomb exploded in a parking garage adjacent to the courthouse.

Using a robot, authorities searched for a possible second device, but by midafternoon had not found another bomb.

Investigators from the Federal Bureau of Alcohol, Tobacco and Firearms were dispatched to investigate the blast and determine if it might be linked to a series of bombings during the last three years.

In the wake of Thursday's bombing, local authorities have increased security for public buildings. The National Terrorism Advisory has not issued an elevated or imminent threat alert at this time but encourages citizens to maintain a heightened level of vigilance.

# THIS AFTERNOON

I need to find a mailbox so I can take my letter, my last message, out of my pocket and slide it into the slot. It will be postmarked from this place, and that matters. My blood connects the past and today. It connects all Da's work with my moment. Today is a very important day. It is exactly one year since I went home and it wasn't there anymore. It is exactly one year since the last time I saw my Da.

I need a mailbox, and I need water.

As long as I'm not dead, there are going to be problems like this.

I'm going to need to drink and eat and sleep.

And I'm going to need to get rid of these stupid silver shoes. Whatever the purpose of shoes like this, walking is not part of it. I had blisters before I made it halfway to town. Now the blisters are broken and turned into little, bloody patches of hurt. So I have to ignore that. It's important not to limp, because limping is something people notice. It's important not to visit convenience stores — not even to use the toilet. Those People have surveillance cameras. And it's really important to find water.

There's a school, and little kids are streaming out of it like chickens out of a pen. Schools have bathrooms. Schools are not quite as surveillance-oriented as convenience stores. I wait until the playground is nearly empty before I go forward and test a door. It is locked. But there are still children leaving, the slow ones. I just catch the door before it closes and I'm inside. I could blow this place up. There are probably still teachers in here. And slow kids. It's an opportunity worth considering, but first I'm going to find water.

When I look up from the water fountain, there is another straggler trying to figure out how to get out the door. This one has his jacket in his teeth and a backpack drooping down to his butt. I could probably stuff the kid into his own pack and zip him up, safe as a turtle. But the burden preventing his escape is the thing he's cradling in his arms. It looks like a dolphin with a circular saw blade stuck in its jaw. Standing on its tail, it's a couple of inches taller than the kid. Since his hands are full, the kid is trying to push the door open with his forehead. It isn't a good plan.

"Need help with that?" I say.

"Yeah, kinda," says the kid.

"It can't be easy to carry a monster like that around."

"It's not a monster. It's a Hee-lee-o-koe-pry-on. It's a real thing."

"Sorry. I just never saw one before. It looks like a fish eating a circular saw blade."

"It's not eating a saw. Those are its own teeth. They grow like that."

I reach out and touch the teeth, which are pointy triangles of plastic — maybe from a milk jug. "You made this? You've got a good imagination."

"I made it. But it's real."

"I haven't seen any around. Where do they live?"

"It's extinct. Like a dinosaur."

"It's a dolphin dinosaur?"

"Not a dolphin. Not a dinosaur. A shark. A prehistoric shark."

"Can I help you with it? Your helicopter shark?"

"Hee-lee-o-koe-pry-on," says the kid, and he lets me take it. It isn't heavy. It's hollow, nothing but air covered up with paper and glue and paint. It has marbles for eyes, shiny and black as the eyes of a frozen mouse. "My brother is going to pick me up in the parking lot. So I just have to get that far."

"Do you think your brother could give me a ride, too?"

"Eric likes to drive," says the kid.

"Works for me," I say, and then I follow him, carrying his real shark thing in my arms like an ugly baby. I can read my new friend's name on his backpack. He's Corbin.

"Hi, Corbin," I say. "I'm Valley."

## Seven Years Ago

Tarzan is just a little boy, little as us, but he discovers how to open the door to the cabin. He's the strange white ape, the only one smart enough to understand, the only one curious enough to try. Tarzan proves you can be little and still be strong. He doesn't care about the dead bones, not even the baby ones in the cradle. Dead bones just don't matter to Tarzan.

He finds books and he studies the bugs — he calls letters "bugs" — they do look like bugs — until he can read.

He finds a knife, and that changes everything.

He is Tarzan. He is a great killer. None is mighty as Tarzan.

We are Tarzan, too.

Bo and I learn to speak Tarzan Talk.

When we wrestle, I say, *"Kagoda?"* Do you surrender? while I bend Bo's little finger back.

*"Kagoda!"* I surrender! says Bo.

Our den is *zukat,* a cave.

Our den is *wala,* our nest, our home. *Wala* sounds like Valhalla.

When we go to sleep, I say, *"Abalu, gree-ah."* Brother, love.

Bo says, *"Zabalu, gree-ah,"* Sister, love.

# Seven Years Ago

## HUMAN SKELETAL REMAINS FOUND IN THIMBLE CREEK AREA

Authorities are investigating after berry pickers found human remains in the remote Thimble Creek drainage in western Montana.

"At first they thought it was just a deer, but then they saw part of a human skull," said Sheriff's Detective Miles McKinley. According to McKinley, the bones had been scattered, probably by predators. Police search of the area recovered a shoe and a clothing label that indicate that the remains were those of a female. Remnants of a sleeping bag were also discovered on the hillside.

The county sheriff's office says the group found the remains on Saturday. No identification was found at the scene, and the cause of death has not been determined.

"It is possible that this is just somebody who went out camping and ran into trouble. At this point, we just want to figure out who it was. We don't have any missing persons linked to the area. We are hoping for a DNA match, but those bones have been out there for years by the look of them, and animals have chewed them up some. Still, DNA, that's pretty much all we got to go on right now," said McKinley.

# Seven Years Ago

## HUMAN BONES FOUND NEAR THIMBLE CREEK YIELD DNA SAMPLE

The County Sheriff's Office now has a DNA sample from human remains discovered last summer, but the sample did not match anyone listed in the national missing persons registry.

A family picking huckleberries found the bones in the Thimble Creek drainage last August.

McKinley says that the sheriff's office is asking the public for help. "She was an adult woman, age 25 to 40, a little over five feet tall. There's someone out there who can help us," McKinley said. "We just need to have them give us some additional information. We've got pieces of clothing and the sleeping bag. We've got the bones and the DNA. Now we are waiting for a call. Somebody out there knew this woman. She has a family somewhere."

According to McKinley, authorities handle more than one thousand cases involving unidentified human remains each year. "People think DNA means case closed, but it doesn't. The DNA needs to be matched with something. We didn't get a hit in the missing persons. There's another 3 million profiles in the joint FBI/state database, but there's a backlog of two years for ongoing priority cases. A cold case like this one, it could be a lot of years before it gets run. Even then, she might not be in there, either."

## This Afternoon

In the next ten minutes I learn that Corbin is in second grade, he's going to be a scientist — a pay-lee-on-tol-ee-jist — and his mom doesn't get off work until seven tonight. When the brother shows up, he gets out of the car to help load the helicopter shark into the back seat, and Corbin says, "This is Valley. She helped me."

He's a taller version of little Corbin, scrawny and spindly. His hair flops down in front and hides the world from his eyes. When he brushes it away, I can see smudges and smears on his glasses. He might as well be blind.

"Hey, 'm Eric," says the driver, and he sticks his hand out to me. It's not the worst handshake. It's not pathetic, but I notice his hand is softer than mine — it feels like there is only gristle where the bones ought to be. I could twist his fingers until they broke, but I don't think I will need to do that.

"Maybe I can just borrow your phone? I need to call my uncle and tell him where I am."

He fishes a phone out of his pocket and hands it over.

"I haven't used one like this. What should I do?"

He takes the phone back and touches the screen. Nothing happens.

"Forgot to charge it," he says.

"Mom is going to kill you, Eric," says Corbin. "He's *always* not charging his phone. And not taking out the garbage. And he *sleeps* in his jeans. He's a total hobknocker. . . ."

"Shut up, Corbin," says Eric, and he wraps a skinny arm around his brother and claps a hand over the noisy mouth. It's an automatic reflex. He's had a lot of practice with that maneuver.

"Can we go to your house?" I say. "I need to call — and use a bathroom."

"I guess."

Things are coming together. I've got a ride I can control. And I've got some time to think. And I can always break his bones if I need to.

# Six Years Ago

Kerosene casts a warm, yellow bubble of light around the three of us. The nights are growing longer, as they always do when the air grows colder. Bo and I know about the seasons, just like we know how to balance the equations. Da explained it all to us long ago, on a night like this. He drove a screwdriver through an apple, which he said was like the Earth. Some things, he said, are difficult to see because of where you are. One thing that is difficult to see is that the Earth is unimaginably big and the sun is much bigger than that. This apple, he said, is like the Earth, and the lamp there is like the sun. Every day the Earth spins around like an apple on a screwdriver; every year it walks in a big circle around the sun. Sometimes the apple is farther away from the lamp, and that is when it is winter. There is some wobbling, too, that the apple does as it spins, and that makes the days shorter and longer. And then Da peeled the apple with his knife and fed each of us slices off the point of the blade.

We were silly little kids then, Bo and me, and after we ate the apple, we turned around yelling, "Day! Night! Day! Night!" until we got dizzy and wobbled. Da said that was enough of that. "Be quiet or I'll knock you quiet."

When we were quiet, we could hear the coyotes talking outside in the cold.

I remember that night, because this one feels the same way.

We sit at the table eating smoked salmon and dried cherries.

Da has covered the table with paper, a clean surface, and the pieces of a clock are all spread out there. The light of the kerosene lamp shines and catches on the inward turning of the flat spring, on the tiny fingers of the cogs and gears.

Da says, "While I was working, a voice came to me and talked to me, and what the voice said, it was true. The customers I work for, they are each a piece of the works. That's not how they see it, though; far as they know or care, they are the whole story. But the voice talked me through it and *I* can see it. I know they are each like a part of the windup. It is my job to put them together so it ticks, so the alarm goes off.

"I haven't been doing that. I just sold them what they wanted so they could send messages about abortion or bad laws or whatever their corner of truth is. I never gave two hoots and a damn about any of their ideas. I just took their money and gave them my expertise. It works out pretty good for everybody concerned. Nothing about that has to change. I will still make their messages. The customer will still get the satisfaction of making their point. But I can make sure those messages speak for us, too. From now on, the messages will all be part of the windup. I will make sure Those People know that."

Da picks up the clock's spring and turns it over in his hand. He holds it out to me, I reach out, and he drops it on my palm.

"From now on, we will send letters, plain paper letters, after each customer's message. The letters will go through the regular mail. We will tell Those People things nobody but us knows about how the messages were built. We will make sure they talk to each other. Hell, we'll give them a list of people they should be talking to. And even with all that, especially with all that, they won't know who we are, because the customers don't even know who we are. And the beauty of it? Those People will be afraid. We will be showing them exactly how to be afraid. We will wind them right up.

"Valley will write the letter, because she writes beautifully. She will be the only one who touches the paper or the envelope. She will put a spot of her own blood on the message each time. That will be the signature. They can test that blood and know for damn sure that all the letters come from us. And they still won't know who we are. Then, once we get Those People all wound up, we will sound the alarm. People will wake up.

"There is one sad thing about this. It means Valley can't come out with us into the world anymore. The voice said there can't be any trace of her where they can find it. Not one hair from her head, not one speck of blood. So from now on, Bo will help in the outside, and Valley must stay here, at the den."

I look at the flat spring in my hand.

The flat spring is part of the windup.

The flat spring holds the tension.

Is the flat spring lonely?

If it is, it doesn't say.

I am quiet too.

# THIS AFTERNOON

Corbin opens the cupboard and puts two bowls on the counter.

Eric whacks him on the back of the head with a spoon, then he drops it into one of the bowls. "We have a guest."

Corbin gets a third bowl.

"You want something to eat?" Eric pulls a box out of the cupboard and shakes it. It's Honey Nut Cheerios.

"Yeah. Yeah, I do."

The brothers walk to a brown leather couch and flop down, one at each end. There's room for me in the middle, but some milk got splashed when they took their places. Eric looks at me standing there with my bowl in my hands, and then he looks at the spot on the couch. He leans over and wipes away the wet puddle with the tail of his T-shirt. The bowl in his other hand tips and milk sloshes out, carrying a raft of tiny cereal life preservers with it.

A fat dog arrives to lick up the spilled food. It's easy to see why he's so fat.

"Got the clicker," says Corbin, and the TV is on.

Eric reaches across me and snakes the remote control out of his brother's lap and into his possession.

"Hey, I'm watching that," says Corbin.

"You've seen that a bunch of times. The candle on the birthday cake is dynamite. The mouse always wins. The cat always loses. Anyway, the Beaver Trap blew up; it's a pretty big deal. I bet we made the cable news," says Eric.

"News is dumb," says Corbin, and he slurps the last milk out of his bowl before he heads for the kitchen.

When the channel flips, Eric's right about the cable news. A dark column of smoke boils into the sky from the place where the Beaver Trap used to be. Then the scene switches to a pale girl, wide-set blue eyes staring at the camera. She is wearing a black vest. There are bright messes of color behind her. Red, white, and blue. Red, white, and black. Yellow, black, and green.

". . . claiming responsibility for the incident," says the news anchor.

I look at Eric. He's stopped chewing. There is a trickle of milk running down his chin. His glasses are smudged, but I guess they are clean enough that he can see the TV, and he knows what he's seen. We made the cable news alright.

"Please," I say. "Eric, I'm in trouble. I need help. Help me. Please."

# One Year Ago

Bo brakes the bike fast. He's teaching me another lesson in alert and ready. I don't want my leg caught under there if he lays it down. He doesn't. He just full stops and kills the motor. Then he points.

There's a clot of black smoke smearing away on the wind. Single-point origin, not a wildfire, at least not yet, nothing to fear. Except Bo's back is tense, and he's hissing at me, "We gotta get off the road."

Yes. Precaution. Sometimes they send out helicopters when there is a fire. Then I figure out it's worse. Where that smoke is rising, that's home.

I want to hurry. I want to know. Bo doesn't ask what I want; he just pushes the bike to the edge of the road and then down the steep bank into the brush under the trees. I trail after, slithering backward down the bank, covering up the tire tracks and the traces of my own footsteps. Those People might find our path if they are looking and they know what they want to see, but they are stupid. We are invisible to stupid people.

Moving the dead-silent bike up and down the steep hills isn't an option. Finding a place where nobody walks and nobody will see it is the best plan. It isn't hard to do. We leave it under a deadfall deep in the ninebark brush. It's only a few hundred yards from the road, but it passes the "what you can't see can't see you" test.

Without the bike, we can move faster. We follow the deer paths when we can. Bo's got the point. I follow his lead. It's still a training day and asking questions is a violation. Bo can hit me if I ask questions. He's authorized to do that when he has the com on training days.

Bo gives me the belly-crawl gesture before we get to the top of the ridge behind the house. We aren't going to stand up there, all obvious. Not until we know for sure what's happening. So far, all we know for certain is there is black smoke rising. If the fire had moved into the trees we would have known. The smoke would have changed color and there would be more of it, but there is less smoke now and it is still black as a tire. Maybe that's it. Maybe Da just built a tire fire as part of training day for me. I check behind me, all around me. If Da is sneaking up on me, I want to be looking. That would make him smile.

Bo kicks me in the shoulder. I should have been looking at him. I should have been alert and ready, but looking at him. He points at his eyes and makes the sign for binos. I dig them out of the pack and hand them up to him. He gives me a stay sign and crawls forward to see what he needs to see.

It takes a long time for him to see what he needs to see.

"They've come," Bo says. "Those People are here."

When I crawl forward on my elbows, I see for myself. The house is still burning, but they are pouring water on it. They are guys in yellow slickers. They are guys with uniforms and guns. They have fancy hats. They have rigs with stars on the doors. They have a big red truck that pumps water. I don't see my Da anywhere, but maybe they have him trapped in one of those rigs. Maybe he is chained up with handcuffs. I know maybe they killed him. I know that maybe. He always told us this day might come.

We know what to do.

What we do now is wait.

We have to wait.

We have to be invisible.

We are prepared. We have food and water and emergency blankets to stay warm. We have knives, and Bo has his hand weapon. We have those things because we always have those things on training days.

Da told us this day was coming.

# THIS AFTERNOON

"We can take you to the police. The police can help." Eric keeps his voice soft and quiet so Corbin won't hear.

"No. Not the police. They won't help me. Trust me. I just need a ride. *You* can help me," I answer in my own secret-sharing voice. When I look at his face, I can see he will do it. He will help me. He *wants* to help me. I just need to give him one more little nudge. "My brother is depending on me," I say. "My brother . . ." That's when Eric takes a deep breath and nods yes.

"Corbin," I say, loud enough that the little one can hear me in the kitchen. "Your brother is going to give me a ride now. . . ."

"Hey, yeah, I want to come! Eric, you can't leave me. You know. Mom says you got to stay with me."

"Sure. That works, right, Eric?" I don't wait for Eric to say anything. "But, before we go, you should go to the bathroom and get us some snacks for the road. OK?"

When the little brother trails down the hall, I turn to Eric and say quietly, "It will be OK. It's fine if he comes. We just don't want him to get scared and confused. It's just a ride. Nobody knows I'm with you. Nobody knows where I am. It's just a ride. Right?"

Corbin is back in the kitchen now, rustling around in the cupboards.

"I like snacks. Get us lots and lots of snacks. And something to drink, too," I tell Corbin. I turn to Eric and say, "Do you have gas? I can give you money for gas if you need it." His answer will tell me if I've got him under my finger, if he's ready for me to push him where I need him to go.

"I have gas," says Eric. "And anyway the gas station was by the Beaver Trap. It blew up." It is a very normal thing to say. He's keeping our secret. He's protecting his brother. That's very good.

"Oh, yeah. Wow," I say. "Gas tanks blew up like crazy. Blew up like a bomb. Well, good thing your car is ready to go then. But I still want to give you money for your trouble."

I notice a chessboard on a little table by a window. The board is dusty. This game has been sitting a while. I reach out to put my finger on the queen nearest me.

"Don't touch that!" says Eric. I pull my hand back. What is happening in my pawn's little round head?

"Whose game?" I ask.

"I'm playing my dad."

"Are you white or black?

"Black. I'm black."

"You win on the next move. You know that?"

"There is no next move."

"You want me to show you how?"

He says nothing. He looks away from the game to where his brother is banging cupboard doors, getting ready for an adventure.

"Got what we need? 'Cause let's hit the road." I say it loud, to Corbin in the kitchen.

Corbin grins and shows me the grocery bag he's filled with junk food. I walk over and look in like I'm interested. Calories are calories. A drink is a drink. I choose a knife from the knife block in the kitchen. It's short, a paring knife. The blade is a tapering triangle, dull edged, but strong. It wouldn't be great for peeling apples, but it will be great for jabbing. The point will go in fast and hard. I won't be peeling apples.

# LAST FALL: SEPTEMBER

Even though we know the hillside, it's dead dark and hard to see, hard to put a foot exactly right every time. Sometimes there's junk on the trail. Junk that wasn't there when we left yesterday morning. Bedsprings, those are bedsprings, from a bed that used to be in our house. Something rolls out from under my foot and I fall until I catch myself. Something jabs my hand. It's glass. Just a little piece of glass. I'm hardly cut at all, but, now I know it's there. I notice the crunch of broken glass under my boots. It used to be a window. Now it's just pointy teeth scattered on the hillside. Nobody will ever look out that window to see if trouble is coming ever again. Trouble came.

If Bo and I were home, there would have been three of us. More eyes to see. More hands to fight. I wonder what that would have meant. Then I hear words in my head that sound like Da: "You were following orders." The words in my head are right. We were following orders.

We still have orders to follow. We are at the bottom of the hill. Two days ago we would have been standing beside the back porch. Tonight we are walking past a stinking black place crowded with burnt things and nothing.

The root cellar is cut into the bank of the hill over there. In daylight it looks like a woodpile with a tarp over it from most directions. You can only see the plank door if you go behind the stacks of split wood. If you do go back there and open the door, all you see is a hole in the ground, some board shelves with cans of food and some jars of things Mabby canned before she died. We never ate that food. It's too old to eat now. We don't put food in the root cellar anymore.

When Bo pulls the door of the root cellar open, it smells like dirt and wet. It doesn't smell like smoke. We pull the door closed behind us. Bo finds the flashlight hanging on the back of the door. He cranks it up and the light shoots out onto the dirt floor. He hands it to me. Part of me wants to look at the words Mabby wrote on the jars: PEACHES, CARROTS, PICKLED BEETS. Sometimes in the summer, I come in here where it's cool and dark to look at the letters my Mabby wrote. It helps me remember that she was real.

I can't read the labels now. Bo needs the light to see, so I shine it where he is working. He shifts some plastic milk crates full of rusted hinges and parts that don't fit anything. He moves some boards leaning up against the back wall. He steps aside, and the beam of light threads down into the tunnel. This is the back door to the den. This is the way out Da made. Da might be in there, waiting for us.

We need to go find him.

There's a med kit in a coffee can on the shelf. We need that. I hand the flashlight to Bo. He moves fast to the first turn point, then he keeps going, silent. I follow in the dark. I know where I'm going. It's like getting a cup of water in the middle of the night. I've done it so many times.

Then the light swings back on me and makes me blinder than the dark ever did.

"He's not there," says Bo. "It's caved in at second turn."

Da probably got out before the collapse. He didn't need the med kit. That's what I think.

When we get back to the root cellar, Bo pushes the few last jars of food Mabby left behind out of the way. Behind them, there are other jars. Nothing says what's in them, and you can't tell by looking because they just look black. One, two, three, four, five. All there. Da never took a jar, either. He might have just been in a hurry; that's what I think.

Bo picks up a jar and unscrews the lid, and then he dumps it out on the floor. Inky water and another, smaller jar. He opens that jar. There's a little kiss of air when the seal breaks. There's a neat roll of money inside, just like Da stashed it. Five jars, five wads of money. The money and the med kit go into the backpack. The jars and the lids go back on the shelves. The boards and the milk crates cover the entrance to the den. We turn off the light and wait for our eyes to adjust. We open the root cellar door and step from the darkness inside to the darkness outside.

The air smells bad. The smoke has all blown away, but the smell of burning is thick as snot. It makes my eyes water and my nose run.

Before we leave, we have to retrieve the intel from the job shed. The padlock is still on the door. That's a good sign. The little twig jammed in at the top corner is still in place. That's a better sign. Nobody but us would know to look for that. If Those People opened the door and then locked it up again, they wouldn't have known to put the twig there as a sign.

I squat down and wait while Bo goes inside. It doesn't take him long. Everything is always ready to go — the intel, the solar, the gun, the ammo — all in one package. Bo's got it. He locks the door. He puts the twig back. If Da comes, he will know we were there. He will know we have the intel and everything is safe.

We have everything. It's time to get out.

One thing I wish we had is the night-visions, but they were in the house, and now the house is gone. I wish we had the night-visions not just so we could move through the dark faster; I wish we had them so I could look at what's left of my home. I wish I could look at that, and really see it, because what I can see doesn't make any sense to me. Maybe if I could see in the dark, I could know what happened better.

I walk over the flat rock that was the front step, and I stand on it.

If I opened the door that isn't there anymore, I would have been in the kitchen. The grey enamel coffee pot would have been on the stove. I think that shape used to be the stove. I step to it and touch it. It still holds the warmth of the fire, even though they doused so much water on it. It was made for fire, but fire on the inside. When the floor burnt out from under it, it fell over. I squat down beside it and remember how I used to put my socks in the warming oven in the winter. Warm winter socks in the morning. I wish morning would come and I could climb down the ladder from my loft and put on my socks, warm socks.

"Valley, we got to go," says Bo.

And we do.

I'm disappointed when we come to the gate of the retreat property and it's locked and twigged, but Da would have locked it if he came this way. And he would have twigged it, too. Da is always careful about the rules.

So I'm optimistic again while we take the bike down the rutted dirt to the place where the bus is parked under the trees. I'm optimistic until I can't see any smoke rising from the stovepipe sticking out the bus window. Maybe Da isn't cold. That's good, if Da's not cold. That means he's feeling strong. But when we stop the bike's engine and there is still no Da, no smiling Da, then I have to start being optimistic that he will be getting here when he can. I have to remember that we had it easy. We had the bike for transportation. Da is having to figure things out. That can take time.

Right now, we're tired, but that's OK. We're home. This old school bus is *wala* for us, a den, a home. Da brought us here often enough to know the area — not often enough for anyone to notice that we were here.

We build a fire in the little barrel stove and we dip into the water supply to fill the coffee pot. Pretty soon it's on the boil. We just stand by the fire and wait. I get the front side of my body as hot as I can stand it, then I turn around and toast my backside. We open bags of food, add some of the hot water, and stir them up. Mine is gloopy and orange: lasagna. Bo's is gloopy and tan: stroganoff. I eat a few bites before I break down and go to the metal storage box and pull out a bottle of corn syrup. After I stir some of that in, it tastes just like home cooking. Bo smiles and does the same.

We are warm, our bellies are full, and we are safer than

we have been in days. We can sleep now. When we wake up, we can check the intel for our orders. That will be soon enough.

"I'll take first watch," says Bo. It's still daylight, but sleeping is going to be easy.

"Four hours," I say.

"Hey." Bo is shaking my shoulder. Judging by the moon, he let me have more than four hours. I'm grateful to Bo. He takes care of me, and I take care of him. That's why we are us.

I crawl out of the sleeping bag and he crawls in.

One of Da's wool shirts is hanging on the back of the driver's seat. I wrap it around me. The sleeves are way long, nice and cozy against the early morning cold.

I push the lever that opens the door of the bus and the doors flap open. I step out into the nearly dark world. Something happens to light when it bounces off the grey mirror of the moon: all the color bleeds out of it. It's a world of grey-and-dark, grey-and-light that the moon shows me. There is a pair of night-visions if I want to get them. Da always made sure the bus was stocked with essentials, everything we would need. I don't bother with the night-visions though, because keeping watch at night is more about listening than seeing. Even though my ears aren't as good as Bo's, I know paying attention is what matters. What I can hear now is the air moving through the needles on the trees and the squeak of one branch against another. I tuck my nose into the collar of the shirt. I can smell my Da. He's as close as the smell of wood smoke, sweat, and wool.

The computer is charged, but we wait until the sun is up so we plug it into the solar collector for a trickle charge before we turn it on. Never waste an opportunity to conserve resources.

Bo and I sit shoulder to shoulder sharing the screen. We open the file named TROUBLE/SEPTEMBER. Da is talking to us. He recorded all the things we didn't need to know until now. Five minutes later we have the intel we need for the next month. Now we just start counting off the days. Checking things off the list. When Da gets here, everything will be exactly as it ought to be. If he doesn't get here when the month is up, we come back for the intel in the file named ACTION/OCTOBER.

Today's list is a short one: Settle in, scout for wood, play chess, be good to each other.

It is very comforting having our Da with us this way.

# THIS AFTERNOON

It's crowded in the back seat. The helicopter shark thing is still there — so are Corbin's school backpack and his sweatshirt and a load of other crap. Now we add Corbin and his bag full of drinks and snacks. The fat dog goes in the back seat too. The dog is coming along because Hey! Why not?

I perch forward on my seat in the front. The vest is starting to rub the skin off the side of my neck, and it is hot. I tug the zipper on my hoodie, just a little, just enough to be a little cooler. Once the car starts moving, the air will circulate and I'll be able to forget about my body and where it hurts and where it stings.

Eric turns the key in the ignition and says, "Where are we going?"

"Does this car have a computer that tells you which way to turn?"

"This car doesn't have a *radio* that works," says Corbin. "Mom says a radio is a distraction, and Eric should pay attention to the road."

"Your mom is totally right," I say. It would be handy to know what the cops are thinking, but Those People probably wouldn't say the truth on the radio. Radio reports would be a distraction, lies and distraction. I need to trust what I know, not what they want me to know. "That's OK about the car computer thingee, too. *I'll* be the car computer thingee. I'll say where to turn, how fast to go. I'll say everything. That'll be fun, huh, Eric? 'Turn right when leaving the driveway.'"

My pawn Eric does what he is told. Perfect.

# LAST FALL: OCTOBER

It is time to open file: ACTION/OCTOBER.

"You can't stay in the mountains for the winter." Da is talking to us through the screen. "If it hasn't snowed already, it will soon, and you need to leave before you get caught. The bus is roadworthy. I always kept her roadworthy. Bo, you can drive her down. She's bigger than the truck, steers a little harder, but you can handle it. Both of you, these are the things you got to do before you hit the road. Valley, write them down."

It's a long list, very specific. There are jobs for both of us.

"Once you get these done. It's time to come back. Open the file named Castling."

. . .

"What are you doing?" I ask Bo.

"I'm gonna swap this tire with the spare," Bo says while he spins the lug wrench in his hand.

"Not on the list," I say. "On the list is 'cache supplies, take the stove apart, and make sure nothing in the bus can shift around.' That's what we do today. Nothing on the list about tires. Is it flat?"

"Not now, but I don't trust it. The spare is better."

"What about the stove?"

"Gotta wait until it cools off anyhow."

"Not that hot. Fire's been out since last night."

"This won't take long. Done before you know."

I don't see the point, but it's not my call. Bo's still got the com. I'm going to cache the supplies, just like it says on the list. The wind blows cold on my neck while I walk off with my sealed plastic bucket that holds 25 percent of our cash money, two handguns, ammo, a tarp, MREs, and a field first-aid kit. I'm going to put it in the place it belongs so it will be waiting if we need it.

Bo is sitting on the tire when I get back.

I wonder why he isn't working, but then I see the front of his shirt is dark and wet. He's holding one hand in the other. The color on his hands shows the wet is blood.

Da taught us how to sew up cuts.

He put a buck's hindquarter on the table and slashed through the muscles with a knife.

"Most the time, you can just tape it shut and it will heal, but if it's a deep cut, that don't work. You can sew muscles together. There's things you can't fix. Tendons, once they snap it's over.

"And live meat bleeds more, way more, so you got to wash it out with saline so you can see. And you don't want to sew no dirt into the cut, so that's another reason you got to wash it with the saline. Hold the edges together with the pointy tweezers. The needle is curved to make it easy to hook through the meat. Make sure you use the needle clamp to hold the needle, because blood makes it slippery, and you have to have it under control. You need to twist the needle just a little to get it to punch through. Skin is tougher than you think, and muscle, muscle resists. You feel that? Don't pull the sutures too tight. There's almost always time to make a knot after each stitch. Keep it clean."

Live meat bleeds more, way more. Right now Bo's hand is live meat, but his fingers are so messed up, the meat isn't even bleeding right.

"That needs washing," I say.

When we get it washed, it looks worse. Those are bones sticking out. One of them looks like it got pulled apart at the joint. That has to be better than the other one. That bone got crunched through and splintered to bits.

"I'm going to have a hard time flipping the bird," says Bo.

"You're lucky it's your right hand." For most people, that wouldn't be lucky, but Bo is left-handed. "What I need to do is get rid of that smashed bone before I try to put it together. You gonna let me get this? I got it."

"Yeah," says Bo.

So I give him some antibiotics and the pills we got for pain. Then I get to fill the little syringe with anesthetic we got from the vet supply store and poke it into the raw meat here, here, here . . .

"Hey! Shit!" says Bo.

"That hurt?"

"Yeah."

"That's weird. I would have thought it hurt so much already. Maybe I actually hit a nerve or something." While I'm talking I'm pressing the tip of my finger on the smashed meat. Bo isn't saying anything about that hurting. It's getting numb. That's good. "It's probably better if you don't look at it," I say.

"I can look at it," says Bo.

"OK. Your choice." I pick up the sharp little scissors and cut off some of the raggedy pieces. It's better to have a clean edge for healing.

When I look up, Bo is staring out the window. He's staring so hard, I bet he can see right through the world to the other side. Then I use the scissors to cut down into the unsmashed meat until I can see the joint between the crunched bone and the rest of the finger.

"Once I get the bone out of there, I can sew them both up."

I use tweezers to pick out the bits, tiny and sharp as the baby teeth of a weasel. The biggest part is still stuck in place, held there by white tendons. I dig the point of my knife blade in and pop the bony sockets apart. It's like butchering a grouse.

I check again for bits of bone. I squirt it with saline. I use the scissors again to trim away scraps of skin and muscle. I bring the clean edges of the meat together, put the needle through, tie the knot. Another knot. Another. Keep it clean. Keep it dry. Take the full course of antibiotics.

"I'm done."

"Yeah." Bo is still looking out the window.

"Go lay down. Keep it elevated."

"Yeah." When he stands up he's a little woozy, but it's only a couple of steps to the bunk.

"I'll clean this up and build the fire. You sleep."

"Yeah."

I pick up the little pieces of bone I pulled out. I rub off the blood. This morning they might have got warm when Bo wrapped his hands around his coffee cup. This morning, blood cells were getting made inside there. That's over now. It's over.

I'm wired.

I wish I could do it all again.

It was interesting — really fun. I bet Bo doesn't want to take another go. It was not so much fun for him.

I burn the mess of soggy, bloody gauze and sterile wrappers once I get the fire going. I drop Bo's finger bone into the deepest, hottest heart of the coals.

That finger's going to get to Valhalla before the rest of him. It's funny. First thing Bo does when he gets to the other side, he flips everybody off.

Bo's a funny guy.


"I think we need to know what's next," Bo says.

He's been asleep for a day and a half. I checked and changed the bandages. I gave him water and pills, but he was never really awake enough to pee. Today, he did that — and he ate food when I handed it to him. And now he's talking. "We should look at the file named Castling."

I look at him with one eye part-closed.

"I know, Valley. We still haven't torn the stove down. We haven't crossed it off the list. But we've lost a couple of days. We gotta take that into account."

We lost a couple of days because Bo didn't stick to the

list. I don't say it, but there it is. I don't say it because Bo has the com. That's the way of it.

It is time to open file: CASTLING.

There isn't enough sun to trickle charge the laptop, so we sit side-by-side on the bed platform at the back of the bus. Bo can stay in his sleeping bag that way. He can conserve his energy.

"Good," says Da. "You're prepped and ready to go."

Not exactly, I think.

"Bo, the bus is sort of noticeable when it's on the road, so you make sure you keep it slow and steady. Now I'm going to give you the directions to where you gotta go. When you get there, you tell Captain Nichols who you are; say, 'I'm Bo White, Dalton's boy.' Now, Valley, you write these directions down. I'll go over them a couple of times so you can confirm."

So Da gives us the directions, and I check them step-by-step.

"One last thing," says Da. "I can't give you the orders you need here on out. The situation on the ground is changing. One of you has to have the com, and the other one has to respect that. That's why I can't just give it to one of you. You have to decide. And the way you decide it is — you play chess. The winner has the com. That's how it will be."

I shut the laptop.

Then I get the chessboard from where it sits on the table.

I set it up beside Bo on the bed. I get a candle, because the light is sliding off the edge of the world and it will be night soon. It will be night before we finish the game.

I hold out my two hands. I do not know which hand holds the white pawn, which holds the black. I hold my hands out and Bo reaches out toward one. I open my hand. It is the white pawn. Bo has the first move.

We are peaceful in the candlelight, playing chess like we have so many times.

But this time is a little different. It matters who wins.

This time, I win.

It's no wonder. Bo is distracted a little bit by the pain in his hand and the pills that keep it from being worse. But he made the move that got him hurt in the first place, so I am the better player where it matters. I win, and that means I have the com.

# THIS AFTERNOON

There's more traffic than usual on the frontage road. That'll happen when you blow up a truck stop by the interstate. More traffic is fine. We fit right in. We are not worth noticing. We are invisible.

I squirm around so I can see Corbin in the back. "The more I see it, the more I like your shark thing. It reminds me of Viking dragon ships. You know about those? They put dragon faces on the front to scare people. When people saw those ships coming . . ."

"Dragons aren't real."

"Maybe not, but Viking dragon ships were real. They sailed places where no one had ever been before. They had adventures. We're like that. We're having an adventure right now. I think we should have Viking names, since we got a

Viking dragon. I'm Valkyrie. You"—I poke Eric's shoulder with my fingers—"Eric's a good start. We'll call you Eric the Boneless." He flinches a little, because I poked him harder than I needed to, but doesn't say anything.

"What about you, Corbin? Who are you gonna be?"

"Crow. His name means crow," says Eric. I guess he's listening after all.

"Corbin the Crow?"

"I don't want to be a dumb bird."

"Personally, I like crows — and ravens. I'm glad to know you, Corbin Crow. But, if you need a name to take into battle, how about Corbin Sharktooth? That's fierce, if you want fierce." Corbin shows all his teeth. He's Corbin Sharktooth now.

I twist myself back until I'm facing forward and pull the zipper all the way down on my hoodie. I'm sweating under my vest. I can't do anything about the weight on my shoulders, but there's no reason not to be more comfortable, to feel a little air. I roll the window down a little. When I do that, Eric glances over. His hands grab the steering wheel tight, and then he glances again. He sees the vest. He *sees* it. I can see him starting to be afraid.

"Don't worry," I say. "Trust me."

"Is it . . . ?" He wobbles his head back and forth. I think he's trying to see his brother in the rearview mirror.

"It's safe," I say. I don't tell him there is more to it than that. I don't tell him that I can touch the trigger. I don't tell him it is my choice when and where and who.

"Can you just take it off?"

"It's safe. I'm safe. *We're* safe. As long as I don't try to take it off."

"Is that why you need to get to your uncle? Wouldn't the police be better?"

My uncle. Ha! I forgot I told him that. "No," I say. "The police can't help us." Does he notice? Does he notice that now I've made it about us, all of us, and not just me?

# LAST FALL: OCTOBER

It's snowing. It might be gone by tomorrow afternoon, but right now snow is dropping in blobs the size of baby birds, or the ghosts of birds, white and disintegrating. This snowfall is heavy — and wet. We could wait. In a few days, we could be driving the bus on naked, frozen dirt. In a few days, we could be having a hard time opening the bus doors because they are blocked by banks of snow. It's a choice. It's my choice, because I have the com.

"We should go." I say, "We let the fire die. I tear down the pipe. We get things packed stable and we go."

Bo doesn't argue.

He helps as much as he can, one-handed.

· · ·

The snow hasn't stopped by the time we reach the black-top, but now it's colder. The flakes are smaller and angrier. Everything is freezing hard. The miles behind us taught us some things. Stuff that was packed secure rattles loose every time we go over a rock or a rut, and the whole road down is rocks and ruts. It's a constant fight to keep stuff from sliding forward. I get one thing stuck tight and then something else comes at me. Another thing I know now is that the wind-shield wiper on the driver's side doesn't work, so when I have a chance I have to climb up on the heater beside the driver's seat and reach out through the window to push away the snow so Bo can see. I'm wet and cold to the shoulder, but that's nothing compared to what Bo has to handle. He needs to shift with his right hand, and that hurts. I can tell by the way he seizes a deep breath before he reaches out to do it.

Here on out, it's pavement, slick pavement, and traffic — and the highway patrol. We are lucky, though. It is getting dark and the road is bad enough that most people aren't on the road. As for the troopers, we see lights blue and red glittering through the ice and wet on the windshield, but they are in a hurry going the other direction. As long as we stay on the road and other people wreck, we've got cover, because the authorities have more pressing concerns.

I believe we have come to the right place. We followed Da's directions every turn and mile marker. I believe we are at the right place, but Captain Nichols doesn't have the welcome mat out. That's OK. That's normal. That's smart. But most people just need barbwire and signs about how willing they are to shoot you to make their point. What I see in the beams of the bus headlights when we pull onto his road kicks everything up a notch. The rusty gate is eight feet tall and sixteen feet wide and filled top-to-bottom, side-to-side with a direct message: KEEP OUT. A barricade like a fortress wall stretches as far as I can see into the night on either side of the gate. If he ever does let us in, we will be deeply protected. That is why Da sent us here. This is the safest place for us now.

Bo turns off the bus. It's the middle of the night. We have come as far as we can without invitation. Now we wait.

Something is hitting on the bus door. It's still dark. "Hey," I say. "Hey, Bo." But Bo is already reaching for the door lever with his good hand. He pushes it open.

All we can really see is the shotgun barrel.

"I'm Bo White, Dalton White's boy," says Bo. "He said we should come."

"Dalton White is dead."

"Yes, sir."

"And you're his boy?"

"I'm Dalton's boy. And this is my sister, Valley," Bo says.

Then he adds, "We didn't know. Not for sure. You know for sure he's dead?"

"I'll open the gate. You pull on in. We'll talk, but yeah, he's pretty for sure dead."

Captain Nichols's computer is big, like a TV in a motel. His house smells like dirt, and not the good kind. But it is warm, and he gives us cups of coffee before he calls us over to stand beside him while he sits in front of the screen. He types in "Willow Gulch fire" and then we can read.

### FIRE, DEATH UNDER INVESTIGATION

Firefighters battled flames and smoke—as well as explosions—at a remote cabin on Willow Gulch Road. An area resident reported plumes of black smoke at 11:30 a.m. Arriving fire crews found a frame cabin fully engulfed. Shortly afterward, several explosions rocked the home.

Two firefighters near the structure were knocked to the ground by the blasts. They were treated for cuts and bruises but were not seriously injured.

Two water tender trucks shuttled water from nearby Little Willow Creek. Suppressive action kept the fire from spreading to other outbuildings or the surrounding forest. Deputies trained at the national fire academy remained on the scene Friday, continuing the investigation into the cause.

There was a picture. It didn't show the hillside or trucks or Them in yellow slickers. It was like looking into the stove.

"You know computers?" asks Captain Nichols, looking at me.

"Yeah, we both know," I say.

"But he ain't much use. Can't bang on the keyboard with that." The Captain points at the blunt wad of bandage Bo is holding near his chest. I should change the gauze. It's been a while since he had pills, and it must have hurt while he was driving.

"Sit you down here," Captain Nichols says, and he pulls out the chair with wheels so I can sit down at the computer. The keys are dirty with the filth of the Captain's fingers. When I touch it, the keyboard feels different than the laptop. It's bigger, and I don't know how to move the cursor. I don't know how to click.

"Here," says Captain Nichols. And he puts my hand on a lump beside the keyboard. "Use the mouse." His hand swallows mine up. He pushes down and clicks, double-clicks. He moves the cursor. He moves my hand. His fingers are blunt. His thumb is wide and thick as a hammer handle.

"Like that," says Captain Nichols. "You got it?"

I make the cursor arrow move across the page and turn

into a pointing finger hand sitting right in the middle of the picture of the flames at the Willow Gulch cabin fire. The picture fills the screen and the video starts to play:

"Thanks for watching this evening. Leading our news, explosions complicated fighting a fire at a residence on Willow Gulch Road. Anna Frank files this report."

"They knew the cabin was a complete loss immediately. . . ."

There are pictures of smoke from a distance, the way we saw it. Pictures of our home, still full of fire. Pictures of the back door resting sideways against a tree. Some guy in a white shirt is talking. "It was a complete loss. When the first unit arrived on the scene, the house was fully involved with fire and it partially collapsed while we were walking up there."

The girl is talking again, she says:

"According to Chief Borglund, there were several loud explosions shortly after they arrived. The blasts blew this debris around the cabin." The pictures of the back door against the tree are there while the girl says, "The explosions may have been caused by propane tanks inside the structure. There were no serious injuries to civilians or firefighters responding at the scene. Water from a nearby creek was pumped and used to extinguish the fire. Chief Borglund says the fire marshal is conducting an investigation, but at this time it's being deemed accidental. He says that the cabin may have been occupied, but declined to give further details at this time. Back to you, Sonia."

And the film freezes again, on the picture of the flames.

"Look here," said Captain Nichols. "Click on this." He points at another link on the page.

## WILLOW GULCH FIRE "SUSPICIOUS"

Fire officials said the blaze at a Willow Gulch cabin was "suspicious" but did not identify a cause. Human remains believed to be those of the owner-occupant were recovered. Authorities did not release his name because they had not been able to contact his relatives. Pending investigation, the area is cordoned, but a neighbor reported the structure was "leveled to the ground." Another resident who had been on the scene said, "Black as that smoke was, you could tell some bad stuff was burning. It smelled bad, *chemical* bad, there's no question about that. Maybe that place was built of railroad ties or something. Never been in there. He lived there alone. He never bothered us, and we never bothered him."

## NAME OF WILLOW GULCH CABIN FIRE VICTIM RELEASED, CAUSE STILL UNKNOWN

Authorities have tentatively identified the body recovered at a fire in the Willow Gulch as cabin owner Dalton J. White, 42. Darryl Barbrady, chief forensic investigator at the medical examiner's office speculated White died of smoke inhalation.

The body remains at the state crime lab in Missoula. Barbrady said that the structure's complete destruction might make it difficult to pinpoint a cause of death. Barbrady added that whatever sparked the blast might never be determined either, but fire officials are investigating.

"Da's dead." I say.

"That's what Those People say," says Captain Nichols. "But yeah, that's what you got to go on. If he ain't dead, he might as well be. They got him, and they want everybody to think he's dead. Sorry, kids. That's the way it is."

After a couple of minutes, Captain Nichols says, "He was a level dealer, your daddy. He coulda used a tinfoil hat maybe, but he was fighting the good fight. And I promised him I'd help you out if you needed it, so that's going to happen. We can talk about that in the morning. We can talk about all of it."

## THIS AFTERNOON

"You ever read books?" I twist sideways so I can see the little boy in the back seat.

"I read books," says Corbin. "That's how I learned about Helicoprion. That's how I learned how all this used to be under the sea. All the way to Wyoming. All the way to Kansas."

"Was that back in the dinosaur times?"

"*Before* the dinosaurs. There were lots of things before dinosaurs."

"And lots of things after."

"Maybe not."

"Well, we're here. And that's after the dinosaurs."

"Not after. Dinosaurs are still around. They're just being birds now."

"Birds?"

Two ravens cross our path, their shadows are a moment on the hood of the car, and then they are gliding into the past behind us. And we are in their past, too, from their perspective. "Turn left at the next road," I tell Eric. I don't say, Turn because of the ravens, the gliding, guiding ravens.

I turn back to Corbin in the back seat and say, "I don't think I'd want to meet any dinosaur bird big as a tree so it could just peck me up like a bug. But you don't believe that, do you? You don't believe in dinosaur birds."

"Not like that. That's stupid. They turned *into* birds. They laid eggs. That's a thing they're alike. And there's other things. Things about their bones and feet."

"Did they caw like ravens? Did they sing? Like meadowlarks?"

"We don't know that. Songs don't leave fossils. There's no bones in noise. Why don't you know that? What kind of books do you read? Did you read any *useful* books?"

"I didn't have any books about dinosaurs. I like books with stories in them. Like *Tarzan*. I read *Tarzan* lots of times."

"I saw a cartoon movie about Tarzan. It wasn't very scientific."

"Hey, Bro, stop bugging her. Check in the pocket of my sweatshirt back there. My game's in there — and some

94

headphones. Why don't you plug in and play? You can even play on my files — I'm totally cool with it. You can see levels you never saw before."

"Sweet!" Corbin starts pawing around in the pile of clothes on the seat. "Got it."

"You can do me a solid sometime," says Eric, but Corbin is already connected to the machine, already gone; his body is already a husk in the backseat; all that's left behind are his twitching thumbs and eyes.

# Last Fall: October

"So, what's your plan now you come down from the mountains? Where you gonna live?" Captain Nichols asks the questions while he pours us coffee. He feeds us eggs too, real eggs, but they are burnt crisp and crinkly around the edges and don't taste so good as I remember.

"We need a place to park the bus where we aren't snowed in all winter. That's what we need."

"How you heat that thing?"

"There's a little barrel stove. We put the pipe out the window. And the kerosene lamp throws a lot of heat. We use that nights."

"Even a little stove needs a lot of wood to make it through the winter."

That's a fact. It's inarguable. It's also true that we, right now, don't have a lot of wood. There's plenty of wood stacked by the root cellar where the cabin used to be, but it might as well be on the moon. We can't go there. We can't go back home.

"What about your momma's people? Would they take you?" Captain Nichols looks at Bo all the time, like Bo is the one to talk to, like Bo is the one with the com.

"We are our momma's people," I say.

"Well, then, your options are pretty limited. You got no decent place to sleep. You got no decent vehicle — you can't drive that bus around, and you can't haul anything bigger than a six-pack on that bike you're hauling on the back of the bus. On the one hand, the best thing you got going for you is that you don't exist — officially. Long as that's true, nobody's looking for you and nobody's going to see you. On the other hand, the world don't know you exist, so they don't care if you freeze or starve." The Captain falls silent then. He just drinks his coffee and stares across the table at an empty chair.

"What happened to your daddy's truck?" Captain Nichols breaks the silence and gets up to fill his coffee cup again.

"We saw it there after the fire, but we didn't touch it. We had the bike. I guess it's still there. It didn't burn," Bo says.

"If you could get that truck. That would be an asset. I

might even be able to find some work for you to do if you get that truck."

"What kind of work?" I ask.

"Well, hauling things, to start. People always need things moved around. Your daddy used to move things for people. That was one thing your daddy did. I can maybe set up some jobs like that for you. If that works out. If you're dependable, then we can figure out what other skills you got that people might need." Captain Nichols nods at Bo's bandaged hand. "What happened there? You blow yourself up a little bit? Your daddy, he never made mistakes like that."

"Bo never makes mistakes, either. The jack broke while he was working on the bus. So that's no mistake. Metal fatigue. That kind of shit just happens."

"Yeah, shit does just happen. That's a fact. Your daddy had some rarefied skills, though. Rarefied skills. And people trusted him."

"Da taught me," says Bo.

"Skills you can learn," says Captain Nichols. "But trust you got to earn."

We wait. Bo puts his bandaged hand on his lap. I know he's a little ashamed of it. I never thought about what people might think when they see his missing fingers. Now we are both thinking about that, about how it might look.

Captain Nichols scoots his chair away from the table and stands up, taller than me, taller than Bo, taller than Da ever was. He takes the hat off and rubs his hair back, then he settles the hat back. That's when he says, "I figure we got to go see if we can get your daddy's truck. I figure it might still be sittin' there. I drive you up there, you drive it back here.

"If that pans out, you can stay here a couple of months to get yourselfs organized. But this ain't no charity outfit. I'll take a commission on the jobs and you gotta give me some rent and — and if you mess with my property, I'll know. You're under surveillance, and I'll see if you pull any shit. That happens, I'll sic every kind of government type on you so fast you won't know if you are in hell or the nuthouse. You hear me?" He sticks his hand out at Bo. Bo stands up like a person, and they shake on it. It's a deal. Everything considered; it's a real fair deal.

# This Afternoon

I look out the windshield and imagine the world the way Corbin said it was, all under water. The sun is going down and the shadows wash like waves across the valley from one hillside to another. The light gets greyer, and I can imagine that the water is flooding up to the sky.

In the distance something small as a mosquito is rising over a hillside. It flashes bright in the moment of pure light the sun is leaving behind as it drops behind the western horizon. Maybe that speck is a helicopter shark that will slide through time and the sky to become a raven, or a meadowlark.

"No! No! Turn around! Turn around now!" I scream, and I hit Eric.

"What the hell?" Eric yells and flinches toward the door.

The dog jumps at my arm, but his teeth don't find me. It is stuck — wiggling and fighting — over Eric's shoulder. Eric fights the dog, fights the wheel, and the car snaps from one lane to the other and back.

"Turn around!" I yell, and I point at the sky where I can see what's coming now. "Black helicopter!"

Eric pushes the dog off him and into the backseat. He cranes down to see the thing coming at us.

"No! No! Don't look. Never look! Turn around!"

"I can't turn here. I can't go the wrong way on the freeway."

"Just go across the middle, just go!" I grab the steering wheel and push it the way I need to go. But Eric pushes back and the car turns, skates across the lanes, and scrapes the metal guardrail beside a steep bank. Eric brakes and the car stops on the shoulder.

In front of us, the black helicopter is moving toward the east, not toward us, please not toward us.

"Don't look! Don't look!" I say it again and again. "Never look at a black helicopter."

"It's not black," says Corbin. "I saw it. It's green and white. It's a rescue helicopter from the hospital."

I rise up and my fist flies over the seat and connects with the side of Corbin's head. Before the dog can take another fly at me, I grab its ear and pin it to the seat. Corbin is screaming and crying. "Shut your mouth or I will kill this dog," I say. I pull the paring knife out of my pocket and push the point at the dog's eye.

"Listen to her, Corbin. Shut up. Shut up now," says Eric.

In the back seat, both the kid and the dog are whimpering.

# LAST WINTER

Bo is on a three-day job.

I sit in the bus.

I'm all alone.

I hold Da's wool shirt against my face, but I can hardly smell his life there anymore. He is fading away. The last traces of him are dissolving into the air. If I had the laptop with me, I would watch the messages he left for us. I could see his eyes and hear his voice. But Bo needs the laptop when he's working. I have to get by on what I remember, so I work on that.

*"Those People will be afraid," says Da. He picks up the clock's spring and turns it over in his hand. He holds it out to me, I reach out, and he drops it on my palm. "We will be showing them exactly how to be afraid. We will wind them*

*right up. Then, once we get Those People all wound up, we will sound the alarm. People will wake up."*

I remember.

*"This is the queen," says Da. "She can move all of these ways."* He slides the piece along the board, back and forth, side-to-side, and corner-to-corner. *"She is the most powerful piece on the board."*

I remember.

When I was alone so much — after Da said my job was to sign the messages in blood, after I couldn't go out into the world anymore — when I was alone so much, I learned to play chess against myself.

At first, I used books. I would play the game the way it had been played by the masters against each other. Doing that, I learned many things. Then, I learned to play truly against myself. When I moved white, I played for white. When I moved black, I played for black. The trick, then, was not getting stuck, not falling into stalemate. The trick was winning. That was hard to learn to do.

I am always, always, always determined to protect my king.

I have to keep the game going. That is when I see. The game *is* not finished. Da's game is not finished.

The King is dead, but he isn't in check.

As long as I'm playing, the King isn't in check. The windup is still good. The energy is there, waiting to be let out. I just have to find a way to send the last message. When that happens, Da will have won the game.

I don't usually speak to Captain Nichols. There's no reason for me to be mixed up in conversations about who and what and why as far as jobs are concerned. That's between him and Bo.

But today I knock on his door and ask, "Can I use your computer?" I want to see again about my Da. I want to find out other things that will help me finish his work.

"You remember how it works?" he asks.

I nod yes and he walks back to that room with me. It's dark except for the light that breaks from the screen when he taps the keyboard.

Captain Nichols leaves the room.

I go to the paper to read about the fire at Willow Gulch.

There is nothing new about Da.

I type in "black helicopters."

There is so much to read, and some of it isn't like what Da said. I decide to not believe things that say there are no black helicopters or that the black helicopters are from outer space. I think Those People do not want the truth to be told, and one way to cover up the truth is to tell lies.

But Da taught me enough to know truth from lies, so I can learn more truth. I follow the links from one truthful thing to another.

There are reports of a growing number of large, unmarked black helicopters. Black helicopters with no distinct markings are being seen daily in multiple states by many different people. It is extremely important that people get VIDEOS and pictures of these sightings.

I cringe when I watch the videos. I can hear the helicopters — pock-a-pock-pock-POCK-A-POCK! — through the computer speakers. It's all I can do to look at them on the computer screen. I have to remember it is like TV. The sharks on TV couldn't bite me when I was little and these black helicopters can't see me, can't hurt me. I have to be brave enough to see this, to know this.

Black helicopters have been flying over my city at sunrise. They travel in groups of three, usually, and fly low, maybe 100 or 150 feet above the ground. My neighbors have seen them, too. The noise wakes people up, but there's never anything about it on the news.

I read so many messages like that one. So many people know what is happening, but the messages aren't getting through.

. . . DEA uses black helicopters also . . .
. . . dark camouflage . . .

. . . no identifying marks . . .

. . . numbers there, but cammoed, you got to be real close to see. Can't see them when they fly overhead . . .

. . . black-op military units conduct operations on US soil against citizens . . .

. . . FEDGOV and its bootlickers just say "conspiracy theorist." The sheeple hear that and go back to their TV trances . . .

I can hear Da's voice: "We will sound the alarm. People will wake up."

Captain Nichols is back. He is standing behind the chair, reading over my shoulder.

I can smell his smell and feel him, there, close but not touching.

"You got a one-track mind, kid." And then his big hand slides down my shoulder and onto my chest. He pinches me there, he grabs me with all of his fingers, and it hurts. When I try to stand, the chair with wheels falls over, and I fall with it. Captain Nichols grabs my hair and the back of my neck. He drags me up and bends me over the desk beside the computer.

There is a picture of a black helicopter on the screen.

His other hand pushes my pants down.

"We need to talk about the rent," says Captain Nichols.

"You owe me some rent." He pushes his thumb, wide and thick as a hammer handle into me. It hurts. I stay very still. Captain Nichols leans over me and says, "I make one call. That's all it takes. I make one call, and the other kid is dead. I say he's dirty, and they will shoot him down. Nobody will ever find him. Nobody will know. Except you. You'll know. You'll know you did it." His thumb is out of my body. "So this is the deal. This ain't no charity outfit. You pay the rent; there's no trouble. You say one word, you try anything, and both of you will be dead. But he'll be dead first. And you'll know it."

I pay the rent.

After I pay the rent, I have to watch the movies. That is part of paying the rent. I have to see her, the girl with white hair and the wide-apart eyes, the girl with that body, pay the rent.

She holds the gun by her cheek. She kisses the gun. She puts the gun in her mouth. She puts the gun inside her down there. She pulls the trigger, but there is no bullet. She pulls the trigger, but there is no bullet. She puts the gun in deeper, deeper and faster.

I have to be brave enough to see this, to be this. I have to see what the world will see when they look at her, when they look at me.

That is what I see her do. The girl with the white hair. The girl with my body.

# THIS EVENING

"Hey, Corbin, do you know about whale sharks?" I say. I read a book about a man called Thor Heyerdahl who built a raft and met a whale shark. Whale sharks are grotesque, inert, and stupid according to that Thor. I'd like to hear Corbin's opinion.

Corbin doesn't answer.

"Hey, Corbin, Corbin Sharktooth," I say, but Corbin just curls his head between his knees. He won't even look at me.

"He's scared, Valley. You scared him."

"You don't need to be scared," I say. "The helicopter is gone. It didn't see us."

"He's not afraid of the helicopter. He's afraid of you."

Eric's words set Corbin off crying, "I want to go home! I want to go home! I want to be home." He just says that over and over. It is really tiresome.

Nobody answers. Not me, not Eric, not the helicopter shark. His voice just shrinks smaller and smaller and he curls himself around the dog. He might still be saying the words, but they are lost now, soaked up like snot and tears in the fat dog's fur.

"Having Corbin with us, it isn't going to make things easier. Trust me, he never stops." Eric is looking at me, not the road, and the car drifts a little until it hits the rough edge and the tires make the rumbling sound that's supposed to wake up sleeping drivers. Eric corrects. Some miles slip by in the empty outside.

"Let him go, Valley. We could just leave him behind when we stop for gas. We're going to have to stop for gas soon. Please, Valley. He's my brother."

"Pull over," I say.

"Here?"

"Next ramp."

"We're, like, nowhere."

He's right. There's no ranch lights for miles. "Next ramp. Just do it," I say.

It comes sooner than I expect. There's a road. It probably goes somewhere. There are mailboxes. That means someone lives here. When I look close I can see a pinpoint of light way out there, where the road is going. There might be other places closer the other way, but there's no telling. The light I can see is the only sure thing.

"Give me the keys," I say. "Now, get him up and get him outside."

"Here?"

"This is where we are. You put him out. You get back in. We leave. That's the deal."

When Eric opens the door, the wind claws its way in. It's blowing hard enough to make the yield sign at the bottom of the on-ramp rattle against the metal post.

Eric opens the back door and the fat dog hops out. It's all the same to a dog.

Corbin looks up at his brother and squints. His glasses are crooked on his face. He must have pushed them around while he was getting the tears out of his eyes.

"Valley, we can't leave him here," says Eric. "It's too cold for him. He's too little."

"He stays here or he stays with us. You decide. It's your brother."

Corbin still hasn't said anything.

"Get it done. Point him in the right direction. Just do it. And get back in here."

Eric the Boneless leans over his little brother and leads him to the edge of the road. He points down, into the barrow pit, down by a barbwire fence. Then he gets back behind the wheel and shuts the door. He doesn't look at me. He just slouches over and rests his head on the steering wheel. His shoulders are shaking up and I can hear him breathing, sucking gulps of air through his teeth. He is crying. We don't have time for this shit. I reach over and poke him with the keys. He puts them in the ignition and starts the engine.

"Turn around and go back the way we came," I say. "Turn all the way around and go the other way on the interstate. We need to backtrack a little. We can't be where they look."

Eric doesn't say anything, but he does what I tell him.

Behind us, distance is making Corbin tiny as a mouse. Then the car turns, and he disappears. It's like he isn't there at all.

# LAST WINTER

"Some people's coming. While they're here, you stay out of sight," says the Captain.

"I'll stay in the bus."

"No, not the bus. Too many windows in there, and it's too near the house. You take a sleeping bag and go on into the trailers. You stay there until they go."

"Can I use the kerosene lantern? It's going to be cold."

"Shit no. Want to burn the place down? Them trailers are flammable. No fire. No flashlight either. If there's any light, somebody might get curious. Might see you. That happens, I'll just pretend you're some squatter. I'll give you to them and have them get rid of you. They'd do me that favor."

. . .

I've never been in the trailers that make the front wall of barricade around the Captain's place. He said KEEP OUT, those are his property. So I kept out. He goes in there whenever he wants, just like he goes in me whenever he wants. His property.

Some places, between one trailer and the next, there's stacks of old washing machines and refrigerators, but mostly, one trailer is right up next to another, overlapping so the back door of one trailer hooks up with the front door of the next. It's a snake made of aluminum houses, and I'm stepping into its mouth. I will have to live in its guts until the visitors go away.

I'm just a pawn. If I don't march along one step at a time, my knight, my brother, my *abalu,* will be lost. The game will be lost. I have to be brave enough to see this, to know this.

I open a door and crawl into the trailer like the Captain says. The roof is caved in over the kitchen. Maybe a tree fell on it when it was someplace where trees grow. Maybe the snow gathered slow and crushing, winters and winters ago. It might make a good barricade, but it gives less shelter than a clump of sagebrush. The wind whips right through, and when it touches me, it steals my heat. This is not the place to stay. I gather up my sleeping bag and crawl along the floor, keeping low. I don't want the Captain to have any reason to complain. I will not be seen.

If it were not so cold, if the wind didn't scrape through the windows, there might still be a smell left behind by those people who lived in this shell once.

I see the visitors park their trucks by the Captain's house. I am motionless as a rabbit while they get out and go into the house. I'm a rabbit with clothes on. I hop from one trailer to the next, always careful, slow and careful, always watching. I stay careful, but moving a little helps me stay warm, or at least not feel how cold I am.

The cold has frozen the air solid.

There are mouse turds everywhere.

In this sink there is dirt, a broken flowerpot.

Electrical wires dangle out of the ceiling.

This trailer is packed with boxes and bags and heaps.

Here is a couch where I could sleep, but the smell of packrat pee is strong enough to stab through the icy air.

It is getting dark. It won't be safe to go forward in the dark. There is broken glass sometimes, nails sticking up, ragged, jagged, rusting metal.

Here, I can look out a bathroom window and see the cars passing on the highway. Even if a driver looked, I would not be seen. I am a small eye in an ugly place that no one wants to see.

I am invisible.

I spread my sleeping bag in the bathtub. I'm out of the wind. When cars go by, I might have little moments of light.

I am not alone.

There is water in the sink. There is a mouse swimming in the water. Or, there was water in the sink, and there was a mouse swimming, but now both of them are frozen. Time has stopped. The clock has wound down. The little mouse claws that went tick, tick, tick are stopped. In the last dim light I can see them, there in the ice.

I take off my mitten and touch the mouse on its little dead head. It died with its eyes open. I can touch its little frozen eye. It's a small eye in an ugly place, and I'm the only one to see.

# TONIGHT

I wish I could lie down and sleep. The weight on my shoulders is dragging me down, pushing my bones into each other, crushing my meat. The vest straps rasp my skin, and the raw places sting. It wasn't made to be worn so long. I was supposed to be done by now.

"Valley? Shouldn't we turn around? You said we needed to backtrack, but how long should we go the wrong way?"

"There isn't any wrong way."

I let that soak in.

"The bombs were meant to work together," I say. "First me, in the crowd. Then the truck, later, when everyone rushes to help. The Beaver Trap was never the plan. That was Dolph's stupidity. Dolph blew it." I smile at my own joke. "My plan was perfect, but I hadn't figured on Dolph. But you play chess; you know how it is. Sometimes a boneheaded move happens and everything changes: all the moves you had imagined ahead — useless. Except everything doesn't change; if the game is still on you still play it to win. You make the next move. This vest is my move. If it turns out I just blow you and me up in the middle of the interstate, that's the way it is. But we can do better," I say. "We can do better. Right now we are just waiting for the opportunity to do better."

# LAST SPRING

"Got a big job," says Bo. "Two days to the pickup, then more than that to the drop."

My stomach aches and cringes up inside me. Inside me. Captain Nichols's thumb, thick and filthy, I can see it wrapped around his beer can.

"You come too, this time, Valley," says Bo. "The customer wants a girl. That's part of the deal."

Why? Why? Why does the customer want a girl? I do not want to stay here with Captain Nichols, but why would the customer want a girl? This is not good.

"You're doing good, kid," Captain Nichols says to Bo. "You're getting a reputation for being dependable. You're earning." Then he looks at me and says, "You're paying the rent. Get back fast. I've got another job lined up for you. Big money. Easy money."

Bo smiles. He is doing good. Jobs are coming steady now.

"I wish you could share the driving," says Bo. "We could cut the time that way. Make more trips in the long run."

Bo is very keyed in to the job thing, now.

"When we get back, I'll ask the Captain the best place to get you a license. You should think about a name. You kind of need to use a name that's like your real name so it's easy to respond when people say it. So I'm Joe, Joe Muller. That's so if we call each other our real names in front of people, it won't seem that weird. They probably won't even hear it."

I know all this. Da said it when Bo got his license. It costs money to get a good one, but a good one is worth it. It's worth paying money for one from the DMV—looks real because it is real—but you have to have a connection inside to skip the proof of identity crap.

I asked Da if I would have one, too, some day. Da said he would teach me in a few years, but no need for a license, not for me. A person only needs a license if they are going out into the world to drive on the highways. That isn't my part. Even if the job isn't part of the windup, the world outside is not a place for me. I have my Mabby's looks. I'm noticeable. The last thing a person wants is that kind of attention.

But now I'm in the outside world. I don't go in any stores. I wear sunglasses. I keep my sweatshirt hood on my head. Even then, I feel people looking at me when we need gas or food. I don't know how to make them stop. I never get out of the truck unless there is no choice.

I'm the navigator. We are getting close to the pick-up zone. It would be easy to take a wrong turn and miss the contact. That would not be good. Bo says he really appreciates the help.

We arrive at the place first. It makes us a little nervous, maybe we did take a wrong turn, maybe the directions were wrong, maybe the whole thing is messed up. I don't say any of the things I'm thinking. Finally, though, we can see dust kicked up by a vehicle coming our way.

Bo's calm. He's done this before. Maybe not here, with these customers, but close enough.

A silver van pulls up with a young guy behind the wheel. A really old guy gets out of the passenger side. He and Bo shake. He hands Bo an envelope, then he slides open the side door of the van.

Three pale blue dresses climb out, long skirts, big sleeves, loose at the waist. There are girls inside the dresses, like mice inside cups. Their little hand paws stick out here, and their little bright eyes peek out there. The old man goes from one to the next, putting his hands on their hair.

The old guy gets into the van. The three dresses move to stand by our truck. The van pulls away.

"Valley," says Bo. "This is Daverleen, TheoAnne, and Teal. We are taking them to Canada." Then he walks to the back of the truck and opens the back so they can climb into the shell. That's where we carry the shipments, and this is the shipment we are hauling.

Night comes, but we keep driving. My job is to keep Bo mostly awake. I'm supposed to do that by talking to him, but, really, I have nothing I can say. We listen to the radio. Sometimes Bo says, "You hear that what they said, Valley?"

"Yeah, I heard," I say, but I don't say the rest of it, which is, "Why do you care, Bo? Why do you care what Those People say?"

Hours later, Bo gives up and pulls into a rest stop. There is no one else there — no car-house mobile homes, no semis. He gets out and opens the back of the camper shell. The three girls are still sitting all in a row at the very back. They could have been stretched out all this time, rocking down the highway like babies in a cradle, but they didn't take the opportunity.

I can tell by the way they step when they touch the ground that their feet are full of pins and needles from being cramped up so long.

The three of them trail off toward the brick bathroom building. Bo nods I should follow. It's no hardship; I'm ready for a rest stop myself.

Inside, all three are hidden behind the stall doors. They are whispering to each other. I don't know why they need to whisper. I don't care what they are saying. If they are planning to run, good luck to them. We are in the middle of nowhere, and those pioneer dresses and the bellies hid under them would have to be a drag on their speed. I suppose they could try to steal the truck, but they'd have to get the keys from Bo or hotwire it.

I don't know why I'm plotting their escape.

I sit on the cold metal seat of the toilet in my stall, and listen to them whisper, but I can't really hear any of the words they say — until they begin to sing.

Their voices echo and wind around each other like the songs of birds before dawn. Birds singing about rain and morning and all the other secrets in their little bird hearts.

When they are finished, I watch them wash their hands in the trickle of cold water — all three of them at once, each touching the others' hands. They never look at their reflections in the dull sheet of metal that serves as a mirror. They can look at each other, I guess, to see themselves.

When we go outside, Bo is sprawled out on a picnic table. He needs the rest.

"Do you want to walk around?" I ask the girls. "Stretch your legs?"

They don't answer, but they pace along the sidewalk that runs beside the parking lot. I trail after them and keep my eyes open for headlights on the horizon, but the world is as empty of people as it ought to be. The last stars blink out and the sky turns the color of cement and then begins to blue. The sun is still below the edge of the world. The fringes of the clouds flash bright and light streaks up.

"Look," says Teal, the littlest one, pointing at the clouds. "It's the fingers of God." Then the sun rises higher and the bands of light fade.

Bo calls out, "Time to go." He's still sitting on the picnic table, stretching after his sleep, if he was able to sleep.

The shipment is obedient, they walk to the back of the truck and crawl in, all the way to the back. Then they take their places, sitting there side-by-side, skirts tucked around their feet, just like they were before.

"We'll get you some breakfast in the next town," says Bo. Then he shuts the tailgate and locks everything up tight. I wonder about those girls sitting there. As far as I can tell, they sleep sitting up like chickens.

"Six meaty breakfast burritos, a couple of churros, three milks, and three coffees," says Bo at the drive-through. When they hand the food over in paper bags, he turns to me and says, "Put the milk and three of the burritos in one bag. That's for them. You can pass it through after we get out of town."

"Are they going to share one of the coffees?"

"They can't have coffee on account of being pregnant — or something. You can go ahead and eat now. It's better before it gets cold."

"What about you?"

"I'll wait until we're back on the freeway, but can you pass me a coffee?"

"Are we going all the way to Canada? Won't we have some problems getting over the border?"

"We just take these to this specified location," says Bo, and he taps the folded piece of paper on the dash. "They got it all set up on that end to pick 'em up and take them home."

"They're going home?"

"Yep, that's where they came from," says Bo.

"What they doing here?"

"Don't know. Don't care. Not our job," says Bo. "And you can pass that food through to them now. Keeping them fed is part of the deal."

I slide the back window of the truck open and knock on the window of the camper shell. The windows on the shell are all covered up so nobody can see in, but the girls riding back there can't see out, either. They slide open the window on their side. I pass the paper bag full of burritos and milk through the hole. They say nothing. I say nothing. Then we both slide the windows shut.

The shipment, one of them, is knocking on the window of the truck. I push it open, and a face is looking at me: TheoAnne or Daverleen, not the littlest one, not Teal.

"Can you pull over? It's Teal. She's got the morning sick. Needs some air."

Bo heard, and the truck is already on the shoulder, already slowing down.

"You got this, Valley," says Bo.

Lucky me.

When I open the back of the truck, Teal, the littlest one, is hunched and waiting to crawl out. She has the paper bag the food came in in one hand. The bag is soggy and the acid smell of vomit is in the air. I put my hand out to help her down, but she holds the bag out to me instead. I take it and fling it down the road bank into the weeds.

Teal crawls out on her hands and knees and then stands at the edge of the pavement.

"Breathe," one of the other girls says from where they are still perched in the shadows.

"It'll pass. It always feels better once you hurl," says the other voice.

Teal is swallowing, and clenching her teeth, but she does what they tell her to do. She breathes deep and slow.

I walk around to the cab, open the door, and say, "I think this one should ride up front for a while."

Bo doesn't say yes.

"I think if she don't, the whole back there is going to be wall-to-wall barf."

"Yeah."

"Up here, she's less likely to blow — and she can open the window if she needs to, there's that."

"Yeah."

So I put Teal in the front and climb into the back. The air only smells a little sour. I stretch out and get ready to fall asleep, like any normal person would in the dark in the back of the truck.

But then one of the chickens says, "You're nice." It's a weird thing to say.

"You're nice," says the other one. "We been talking about it, and you can come live with us if you want to."

"What?"

"You can be in our family."

"What about Bo? Can he be in your family too?"

"Don't think that would work. No. Don't think so."

"Why not? He's nice as me."

"But he's a man. He wants to be out in the world. That's

what men do. That's why I hope my baby is a girl. If she's a girl, we can be together mostly for always. With boys, you never can tell, but they mostly need to go."

We wait, parked on the gravel road beside a long lake that stretches from here to Canada. This is as far as we go. Bo crashes on the truck seat. I'd like to go down by the water and stand by the empty edge where the earth and the sky and the water come together. I would like to watch the ripples kiss and bend around the rocks and see how the wind flutters the smooth back of the lake. Can't do it. If something happens, we might need to move fast, so I sit on the loose gravel by the truck. The chickens are totally quiet in the back; maybe they are sleeping, too. I hear the whine of a chainsaw somewhere. No, not a chainsaw, a bike engine, getting closer.

Might be nothing, but I open the truck door and poke Bo awake. He hears the engine, too, so there's no need to talk.

It's an old woman in coveralls riding a four-wheeler hitched to a utility cart. She pulls up behind the truck and stops.

"This it?" I ask.

"Yeah, probably yeah," says Bo.

"You stay here, then. I'll let them out."

The old woman climbs off the machine and stands

beside it. When I open the back, the shipment climbs out and runs to her. They all hug, but she shoos them toward the trailer.

"Bye, Valley!" Teal waves.

"Valley watched on us like we were her own sisters," Daverleen says. But nobody says anything about me going with them, so I don't have to say no.

Bo waits until the whine of the old woman's engine has threaded away to silence before he turns the key in the ignition.

"We'll go for a couple of hours, then I get to sleep. We'll be back to the Captain's by tomorrow, then I'm going to sleep some more. Damn it, Valley, we got to get you licensed," says Bo.

Maybe he says some more too, but my brain is stuck on one thing. We'll be back to the Captain's by tomorrow.

There are no paths here, not even places where the animals always go because it's the quickest and easiest. Here, every way is open and winding around the sagebrush. Here, there's no place to go: No water calling, no promise of something better. There are no fences, no power lines, not even any jet trails in the sky.

The shadows move as fast as the clouds. The bright wind muffles my ears and makes me pull my sleeves down over my hands. But there is a sound that pierces the wind and pings like radar — ping, ping, ping — until it spills out, calling love out of the air, forging it into a bell that rings like a heart. Meadowlark.

It's been a long time since I cried. I've almost forgotten how. My bones and muscles are a fist around my lungs and heart. I curl down onto myself until I'm hard and heavy as a stone. When Bo finds me, I'm just another rock among the sagebrush.

"Hey, hey, Valley, I'm here."

I'm here.

Bo gathers me against him, and I push my face into his jacket and cry. I cry until every muscle in my body is tired. Then Bo takes my hand and leads me back to where the truck is waiting.

# TONIGHT

"Valley, you don't have to do it."

That's true. I'm a free person.

"Revenge isn't worth it."

I let myself think about that — about revenge. I imagine standing in front of Captain Nichols's gate, waiting for him to come close, waiting for him to think I am squirming under his dirty thumb. And then I would destroy him. But I say, "That's not why I'm doing this. Revenge is a bad reason. It's a small reason. I'm not doing this for me. This is way bigger than me. You don't understand yet."

"Understand what?"

"Understand about the black helicopters."

"Valley. You know I don't believe in them? Right? I don't believe . . ."

"I know. That's why this has to happen. There are lots of people like you, people who don't believe. That's exactly why this needs to happen." The tires go kachunk-kachunk-kachunk on the seams in the road. We are moving closer to wherever we need to be. The gears are all turning. The pieces are all moving. I say, "You are a part of it now. You should know that. Even if you are afraid, you are a part of it. Someday, when people understand, they will remember you. They won't remember that you were afraid; the only ones who know that are you and me, and we will both be dead. They will remember that you were brave. You were brave, and you were a part of it. They will know that you helped me when I needed help. You will be a hero, Eric the Boneless. How about that?"

# Last Spring and Summer

"We should kill him," says Bo, "for what he did."

"No," I say, "I've thought about it, and there is no good plan for killing him. Not right now, anyway. Later maybe, but not now. Not when we get back. He's got to expect we might try, so he'll be ready."

I can see the thoughts crawling behind Bo's eyes, crawling and squirming and hatching like mites and maggots. I can see them, and I know them because my own brain has been itching in the same way.

"Not now. He's a person who knows people. If he turns up dead, some of the customers will remember you. When that happens, it will be just like he said. They will think you are dirty and the word will get around. Much as I hate it, killing Captain Nichols, that's a thing we can't do. We need a different plan."

Bo is still not ready to think about anything but blood.

"What do we have for assets?" It is a direct question that has a right answer, no guessing. It requires thought. I can see Bo's eyes move while he thinks to answer.

"We have the emergency cache. The truck. My gun." I can tell he's thinking about putting a bullet into Captain when he says that.

"What about money? The money you've been earning on the jobs? Is that on you?"

"Captain's holding it. We had a ledger where we kept track. He gave me what I needed for operating expenses. I still got a little of that. The customers, they paid him. I never touched the money." Bo can't believe how stupid he's been. I don't need to mention it.

"The stuff we had, that's all still in the bus?"

"Yeah. I never touched that. It's still where we hid it the day we came down to the Captain's. But right now, we don't have the bus or anything inside it. And I don't see how we can get that back unless we kill him."

"Not the option," I say. "How long do you figure we have before he knows we aren't coming back?"

"A day, maybe," says Bo. "We made real good time on the run. But the customers, he's probably talked to them, so he knows we made the drop. If we don't show up in a day, he'll know something's up."

"Can we go back to where the bus was? We've got the emergency cache there. We could get that and then live out of the truck." Even while I ask the question, I know that would be hard. The world's just not full of food and comfort. It's full of sagebrush, rocks, and weather.

"I don't know if the Captain knows about that property or not," says Bo.

"If we don't know, then it's not safe," I say. "The one thing we have going for us is he doesn't know, right now, this minute, where we are." I look out the truck window as the wind rattles past.

"Valley, I think I do know a place where we could go. They're customers, so the Captain knows about them, but — I don't know. They treated me good. They trusted me when I brought the delivery. Gave me some food and beer. We even did some target practice together with the guns I brought. They were good guys. I just felt it. They were good."

Trusting Bo's gut might be the stupidest thing I ever do. It might even be one of the last things I ever do. But I'm going to do it. Because if they kill us, it will be both of us. If they kill us, it will be quicker than starving. If they kill us, I don't have to see the Captain. I don't have to see the Captain ever again.

· · ·

There are three guys shooting hoops. The court is the road. The hoop is nailed to a tree that leans over the packed dirt and gravel. They don't even stop the game until Bo opens the door of the truck and gets out.

"Hey, Joe!" The one holding the ball flings it at Bo. Bo claps it out of the air. I did not know my brother could do that.

"Hey, Dolph," says Bo.

"Unexpected visit," says Dolph. He's bigger than Bo. His hands are empty; that puts Bo at a disadvantage, even if the disadvantage is only the second it takes to move the ball.

"Not work," says Bo. "I wonder if I could talk to Wolf a minute."

Dolph jerks his head slightly, and the other guys move until one is standing right by Bo. The other lines up with me; it would be a clear shot through the open door of the truck.

"Well, come on in, then." Dolph smiles. "Who you got there with you?"

"This is my sister, Valley. Come out the truck, Valley," says Bo.

I get out slow, and we all walk down the road a minute. Dolph stops and the rest of us do, too.

"It's OK, Valley," says Bo. "Just do like me." He puts his hands on his head and stands wide. One of the guys pats him down. I feel hands on me, too, hands that go where

136

they want and touch what they want. Hands that run up under my shirt and across my skin. Hands that slide up and down the inside of my legs. I don't like it, but I don't flinch.

"Wolf's in the Quonset," says Dolph. "We'll all walk on over there and let him know you're here."

And then we walk through the trees to meet Wolf.

They take Bo inside and close the door, but I don't go. I'm left outside with the guy who patted me down. I turn away from him, away from the door that closed behind Bo. I look down the hillside. I can see sunlight glinting on water through the open spaces between the trees. If I walked that way, would he stop me? Could I just walk there, to the water's edge? Would the water kiss and bend around me and hold me while my heart went tick, tick, tick? Or would that be reason enough to shoot?

The stubborn birds are singing in the trees.

If they have a silent way of killing, it will be my turn soon.

When they have finished, the stubborn birds will still be singing in the trees.

But the door opens and Bo comes out smiling. The man with him is smiling, too. He is tall. Taller than Bo. Taller than Da.

"It's good," he says. And I believe him. "Dolph, show them where to park their truck."

One of the other guys punches Bo in the shoulder. "Hey, dude, we got a bonfire meeting tonight. Stormy is going to be glad to see you again. Damn your eyes."

"This is Valley," says Bo.

"I'm Wolf," the tall man says to me. Things he doesn't say, but things that I see in the way the other men obey: I am the leader here. What I say goes. "Bo tells me you could use a couple hours' sleep. So we'll talk more later, tonight maybe, by the fire, or tomorrow. But for now, get some sleep."

Those are easy orders to follow.

The fire is by the lakeshore. Bo is there now. He is one of the moving shapes, half bright, half dark. I'm not. I am here, at a distance, under the trees. I can watch from here, but I don't shine or show against the light of the fire. I'm a shadow, I'm a tree, I'm a shadow of a tree.

"Why aren't you there, with them?" It's Wolf's voice behind me, where I can't hear so well. I wish now that I had stayed in the back of the truck, in the solid dark, instead of following along to watch Bo. My hand is on the little knife in my pocket.

"I'm not with them because I'm not one of them," I say. I turn to face him, but the light of the bonfire is burned into my eyes and hovers where I look.

"You would be welcome," Wolf says. "There's plenty of beer."

"I don't need beer."

"Humh? You don't have to need it to enjoy it." If I could see Wolf's face, he would be smiling. I can hear a little bit of laughing in his words.

"I don't enjoy it, either," I say. "I don't like the bubbles."

"Here, then," says Wolf. "This doesn't have bubbles." His hand touches my hand and puts a mug into it.

I think maybe it is cold coffee, but it smells wrong. When I sip, it is sharp on the back of my tongue, like the smell of pine pitch on a hot summer day, but it also tastes like berries and bitterness.

"My own elderberry wine," says Wolf, "mixed with mead. Better than beer for you and me."

We stand and watch the others by the fire, and we pass the cup back and forth. We are quiet in the shadows under the trees. I start to feel warm inside, from the wine. I watch Bo and the others. I watch how the sparks fly up when someone throws more wood on the fire. Wolf is standing close enough by my side that I can feel the heat his body makes, but he never touches me except to give and receive the cup we share.

Bo and I go to Wolf and Eva's trailer right at 5:00 p.m., like she said to when she invited us. Eva is Wolf's wife. Bo introduced us at the truck when she visited this morning. She was down by the fire last night, and so were her daughters, Wolf's daughters, Stormy and Sky. They are a whole family.

When we walk past her truck, the engine is still ticking, making the little sounds the parts make when they cool. She must not have been home very long.

Bo climbs up the steps to the front door and knocks. Then he steps back down and waits. I start to think maybe we didn't understand, because nobody is answering the door, but then I start to hear loud TV-commercial music coming from inside the trailer.

Bo steps up and knocks again, harder this time, with the side of his fist. It's not polite to knock like that, but the person inside won't hear it otherwise.

The door opens and it's Eva. "Hey, kids," she says. "Come on in." She is holding a cigarette and a can of beer in one hand while she welcomes us in with the other. "I didn't expect you so soon. Wolf and the girls, they're always late. So I figure everybody's late. Not you two, though."

"Da taught us to be on time," says Bo.

"That's real polite," says Eva. Now she's got one hand for the beer and one for the cigarette. She punctuates her sentences by putting one or the other to her mouth.

Not just polite, I think, also important so a person doesn't get blown up. Time matters. Da taught me that.

"Well, I'm glad you're here," Eva says. "Sit down. Sit down. Soon as Wolf and the girls get here, we'll eat. I wanted to welcome you to the family; so we'll be having a big family dinner together. You want a beer?"

"Yes, please," says Bo.

Eva puts her own beer and cigarette down on the counter by the fridge. She pops the top on a cold one and hands it to Bo. I see the edge of the counter has lots of brown marks where cigarettes have been set down on it and forgotten, but this time she remembers; she picks it up and tucks it in her mouth. "What about you, honey? Thirsty? I think I got some ice tea back there somewhere if you want it."

I shake my head.

"Change your mind, you let me know," says Eva, then she walks over and settles into the couch beside Bo. "Relax," she says. "Make yourself at home." Then she picks up the TV remote, leans back, and puts her feet up on the coffee table so we know how to do that in her home.

"About time. I thought I said be home because we were going to have dinner," says Eva when Stormy comes through the door. "Bo and Valley are here."

Stormy makes a kissing face, maybe at Bo, then turns and heads down the hall.

"I'm calling Wolf," Eva says in our general direction. "He probably lost track of time. He does that." She walks over to the counter and digs around in a purse, but before she finds the phone, the door opens again. It's Wolf.

"Let's eat!" says Eva. "I picked us up a real dinner in town." She pulls a cardboard bucket full of fried chicken out of a paper bag.

"Beer me, woman," says Wolf.

"Always, babe," says Eva while she opens the fridge. After she passes the can over, she yells, "Stormy, get your ass back here. Time to eat."

Stormy comes back and sits beside Bo on the arm of the couch. She leans over and looks in the bucket of chicken, then she turns and takes the food right out of Bo's hand. She holds the chicken bone in her right hand; with her left she pulls Bo's hand to her mouth and licks the grease off his fingers. Bo smiles like that is perfectly polite. It is not.

"Where's Sky?" says Eva.

Nobody answers, because, I guess, nobody knows.

"This is my office," says Wolf. There are flags hanging on the wall behind a big computer desk. The closet doors are open, and I can see boxes full of cables and equipment in there. I guess having those things makes this an office. When they built the trailer, it was probably supposed to be a bedroom. If it were still a bedroom, then Sky and Stormy wouldn't have to share, but I don't think that matters much, since I gather neither of them actually sleeps here very often.

There are shelves along one wall: some books and a bunch of little things. I step closer to look: silver and black dragons with shiny crystal eyes, wizard guys with walking sticks — or magic sticks, whatever those are called — soldiers in grey uniforms, soldiers in blue, and, on horseback, valkyries.

"My chess sets," says Wolf. And when he says that, it becomes obvious. I can see how they are ranked, eight pawns here, eight pawns there. Why one guy in uniform is a bishop and another a knight I do not know. And why the valkyries are knights? Because they are on horses, I guess. But truly, valkyries are like queens. They play the pawns wisely and choose the best. They decide who dies and who lives forever.

"I wanted you to see this," says Wolf. He leans over and taps the keyboard in front of the computer screen. "I got this message this morning — from Nichols. The guy who put us in touch with Bo when we needed some stuff delivered."

Wolf waves at the chair by the desk. "Here, take a look," he says.

There is no way in hell I'm going to sit down and be trapped in that chair. I feel inside my pocket for the little knife I always keep there now.

"He writes that you two owe him money. That you're dirty and untrustworthy. He says if we see you, keep that in mind and let him know."

"We don't owe him money. We don't owe him shit."

"He's a greedy asshole. I know that's true. But what

the hell is the rest of this about? Did you put the cops on him? What?"

"If the cops are on him, why's he sending messages to you? If you believe what he wrote, you wouldn't be here this moment now. You'd have better things to do."

"That is true. You are a smart girl, Valley. And no, I don't think Nichols is telling any kind of truth. He's full of bullshit as the day is long. But I did think you deserved to know what the word is out there. Some people who read it might not be as smart as you and me. Some people might believe it. Thing is, Valley, you are welcome to stay here. Far as I'm concerned, Bo is one of my men." Wolf picks up one of the chess valkyries and looks at it while he says, "And you, Valley, you are under my protection. You belong here, with us. From the first moment I saw you I knew that." He holds the little valkyrie out to me, I reach out, and he drops it on my palm. It is warm from when he held it. "Welcome home, Valkyrie," says Wolf.

I stand by the edge of the lake and see how the water lifts and falls in small panting breaths. I hear it move the smallest of the stones, click, click, tick. A buzzing, it is tiny, no longer than my smallest finger, but much more slender than bone, and it's blue, flashing blue in the sunlight. Bo told me this is not a dragonfly, it is a damselfly. He thought they would please me when he showed them to me. They don't please me, the damselflies, but they remind me of my purpose. They remind me of the black helicopters.

They do not remind Bo of the black helicopters. He has forgotten his purpose — or he has found a new one. I can hear him, now with the others, coming out of the trees and down to the shore. They are so noisy; I don't think they can hear anything but the sounds of their own voices.

I walk in to the place where their path meets the beach. I need to have a moment with Bo to remind him that I have the com, and staying here forever is his idea. It is not my order. It is not our mission. But there is no time to talk to him; I see him come out of the trees and kick his boots away. His shirt is off, and he peels his jeans down his legs and tosses them. For a moment he looks toward the trees, then he turns and runs, crashing through the shallow water before he falls forward, like he was shot in the back.

But there is no crack of gunfire. Nothing echoes, like I have heard it echo, off the steep hills and the sky. All I hear is laughing and yelling. I see Bo splashing farther and farther out into the lake. I did not know he could do that.

The rest of Wolf's men come out of the trees and follow him into the water. Stormy and Sky, the last two on the beach, those two. Stormy is pulling her T-shirt up and over her head. She is very slow about it. I'm close enough now that I can see the red welts like a belt around Stormy's white hips when she pushes her tight jeans down her legs. Then

145

she stands on her tiptoes and spreads her arms wide. The men splash water in her direction, but they are too far out for the spray to hit her or Sky, who is standing beside her, mirroring every motion. Then both girls make squirrel-bird shrieks while they run into the lake and then slide like floating leaves along the surface of the water.

"Hey, Valley girl, come on in — the water's fine," yells one of the men.

"If cold is fine," yells Stormy as she rolls onto her back and floats there, facing the sky.

"It is a little nippy out." A man laughs, and then splashes Sky, who sputters and splashes toward him.

"She can't," says Bo, my Bo. "She can't swim."

"I'll teach you," says Wolf's man, Dolph, and he swims a couple of strokes nearer the shore before he stands up and starts wading toward me.

I turn and walk quickly up the path, into the trees.

I do not need Wolf's man Dolph to teach me to swim.

It is not part of my mission.

Tarzan hated water, but he learned to swim when he had to escape. *"Kreeg-ah! Kreeg-ah, Abalu."* Danger! Danger, Brother! Little Willow Creek was too shallow for swimming. We pretended to learn there, but it was only pretend. I can't. I can't swim, but Bo can. I did not know he could do that. It is another thing he learned to do when he could go out in the world, and I could not.

When I was alone so much, I learned to play chess against myself. Most people, they only know how to play for themselves. I know how to play a much bigger game.

But it made me ready to play chess with Wolf.

"I played chess with your father, Valkyrie," says Wolf. "He did some work for me, oh . . . a long time ago. Sky and Stormy were just little girls then. They left their dolls scattered all over the place in the woods. They always needed more dolls." He moves his piece just as I expected, just as I planned. "Those dolls were always naked. Why is that? Why are those dolls always naked?"

I move my piece. It looks like a smart move, but it isn't. I'll see if he figures that out. Then I say, "They give them to you naked. Dolls. Check," I say.

"And mate," says Wolf as he moves to the place I prepared for him. "Good game, Valkyrie."

He's right. I played a good game. It was a better game than he knew. I could have won that game, not once but three times before Wolf finally did.

"You play a romantic game, Valkyrie." He answers the question he sees on my face. "You are not afraid to sacrifice pieces. I think you would beat most players."

I don't tell him the truth. I could have won. I let him win. I don't tell him that because the game I am playing is bigger than he knows.

The King is dead, but he isn't in check. As long as I'm playing, the King isn't in check. He is free. He would want us to carry on. I'm the Queen. I've castled, which is always a risk. But I have my knight in play. And I see Wolf's sideways, sliding glances and diagonal advances. I see them for what they are. I've finally got a bishop. With this piece, I can win.

I watch how things work, and even though there are some details I can't see under the surface, I see. There is money flowing here, flowing in Wolf's direction. When Wolf speaks, people listen — not just the people here, like Dolph. Wolf composes messages — videos, podcasts — and those get heard. Lots of people are listening to Wolf.

That is one thing that happens in the Quonset. Messages get made there, where it is quiet. With target practice, TV game shows, and truck engines, it's hard to find a quiet place, but the Quonset is quiet.

I noticed that the first time I went inside. I noticed the quiet, and I noticed how it felt, snug and cool, like the den. When Bo moved into the guys' trailer, Eva thought I should share the room with Stormy and Sky, but I said, "No, thank you. I'm not used to sisters." I didn't say, Because Stormy and Sky are idiots. There are things that need to be unsaid. I just asked if I could have a bunk in the Quonset, because it is quieter, and I like quiet.

Did I understand that the door would have to be locked?

It only makes sense. There are precious and dangerous things in there.

Really, the locks are a comfort.

When the door is locked, I'm safe inside.

This is my den, my *zukat,* my *wala.*

This is the place where I think of Valhalla.


"Hey," says Bo — or the one that sounds like Bo, but doesn't look right. It runs its hand over the skin that rides tight on its skull, pale, shiny skin, skin that hasn't seen the light of day until now.

"Hey," I say, because what else can I say? Can I say, Who are you? Can I say, You don't look right? I can't; so I just say, Hey, like that says those other things. Like that says, Where are you, brother? *Abalu?*

"I got my hair cut," says Bo's voice. "Eva, she had clippers. Now I look like the other guys."

There's nothing to say to that. I mean, it's truth. But I say, "You look different." That means: People might notice you now. You have given up your invisibility. Why?

Bo says, "Like the other guys."

I don't say, Yeah, like the other guys here. Like Wolf's

men. You look like them. You are invisible here, but in the outside world? No.

What have I got to say about this? My white hair? That's different. The wide distance between my eyes? Different. But my different, that's not my doing. That just happened. I never had a choice. I was born with my Mabby's looks. I was born different. And now, Bo, you are different because you choose to be.

"*Abalu, gree-ah,*" I say. And that means, I see you, Brother. I see you still, and I love you.

"Hey," says the one that sounds like Bo, "there's a keg and fire. You coming?"

"*Abalu, gree-ah,*" I say. And Wolf's man who sounds like Bo walks away, but I stay where I am.


In the kitchen, Eva is trying to smoosh some more garbage into the can, but it's already so full the lid won't close.

"I'll take that and burn it," I say.

"Thanks, hon. It was supposed to be Sky—I think. Never does anything."

"Not a problem," I say, and pick the can up by the hinge in the back. Some stuff slides out. That was inevitable. "I'll make another trip and get this." I point at the stuff that escaped and some pizza boxes leaning up against the wall.

"Above and beyond, sweetheart, that's you," says Eva.

"Maybe you can do a thing for me," I say.

"You don't have to do stuff. You can just ask. You're family now. Wolf and me both said it."

Hearing her say that makes it sound like I was making a bargain instead of just doing my share. My hand is getting tired from standing there holding the can.

"What is it, hon? Just ask," says Eva.

"Will you shave my hair? Like you did Bo?"

"Oh, sweetie, god no! I mean, that would be wrong. Why would you want that? Tell you what — I'll trim the ends if you want. Let's just do that. After you burn the trash, you hop in the shower and wash it, then I'll trim up the ends."

I wonder if Bo had to tell a reason before she cut his hair. I build a fire in the burn barrel and feed the trash into it, little bit by little bit. While the garbage burns, sometimes the flame turns green and the smoke smells of plastic. It all burns; everything I put in there burns. And it all burns for the same reason. When it's done burning, everything is ashes, just like the other ashes.

*When I go to move my knight, my hand is slick with blood. Wolf reaches across the board and turns my hand over. I'm cut to the bone.*

*Wolf touches other places where I am cut open, on the inside of my legs and into my body.*

*"Open it up," he says.*

*And I open my body. I open my ribs so I can see my own*

*heart, but it is hidden under black feathers. It is hidden in thought and memory.*

*And Da comes back. He lifts away the raven's wing, and I see my heart is a flat coiled spring wound up tight, energy bright, trapped in the turnings. He doesn't say anything, but I know the orders.*

*I know what to do.*

When Wolf makes his messages, I sit on my cot and watch. I listen while he talks about his nation within a nation and how it is growing stronger. Wolf's invisible nation is very important to him. He is a great storyteller, Wolf is. He weeps over Ruby Ridge: the mother shot through the head while her baby was in her arms. He rages about Mount Carmel: a bone of a nameless child found in the ashes. The whole time, I'm right there, a visible part of his invisible nation. Then, after he is done sending his message, we play chess and talk.

That is when I set up the plan for Wolf. I tell him my story could be his story.

I watch how he slides his bishop, slippery to the side.

He wants to win, but he wants to lose nothing.

I can make that happen.

I show him the game, little bit by little bit. I show him how to win.

He doesn't say, "Oh, sweetie, god no!" like Eva. He rubs

his chin while he thinks of his next move, then he says, "I see it." He taps his finger on one of the knights that has been lost in the game. He picks it up and turns it over in his hand before he holds it out to me. "You will be our valkyrie."

Wolf has money. He provides the diesel, the fertilizer, the emulsion explosives, and the C-4.

I provide Bo and his expertise. Bo will know exactly what he needs to know about this job, and nothing more. He will not know that I am one of the customers. He will not know that I am one of the bombs he is building. He will rig the trigger I will wear beside my heart.

I have the com. The decision is mine.

Even though I have written messages before, Da always gave me the words. This time, I have to find my own words.

But then, the words don't matter. I could write in the language of ravens or Tarzan Talk. The truth is in the blood, I think. The blood is what they need to read, and the blood is the easiest part. The easiest part is sliding the blade along my thumb. The easiest part is watching the red straight from my heart where it's been wound tight. I have more than I need. I can hear the little drops: tick, tick, tick. There is a certain comfort in this moment when I put the blood against the page. This is the last time.

# TONIGHT

"We're screwed," says Eric.

"What?"

"A flat, maybe, I think we have a flat. I don't know. It's like — harder to steer?"

"Well, pull over and look. What side?" I say. I can't see anything, but it's dark and the side-view mirror isn't set to reflect the tire.

"What if it *is* flat? Then what?"

"Don't be stupid. You know what. When a tire is flat, you change it. You have a spare, right? So if it's flat, you change it."

"Yeah. I guess. I mean, my mom said, if I get a flat I should just call the towing. They're fast. And it's safer that way. But we don't have my phone."

There are a thousand things I could say to Eric in this moment about his mom and the dumb-ass lazy way of living she is teaching him, but all I say is, "We are going to get out. We are going to check the tires. If we have a flat, you are going to change it."

The rear passenger-side tire is flat. Not smack-dab, rolling-on-the-rim flat, not yet, but flat. Eric is standing there beside me staring at it like he never saw such a thing before, and I suppose he hasn't. I suppose it never came up.

"My dad," he says. "He died while he was changing a tire."

"He get hit by a truck or something? You don't have to worry about that tonight. You won't be hanging your butt out in traffic. You'll be way over here, on the shoulder, if anybody comes along." When I say that, the headlights of a car stab us with light for a moment, then the glare slices away and the car blows past us.

"Better hurry," I say. "We don't want to have anybody stop to give us a hand. Get the spare. Get the jack."

Eric pops the trunk and shifts some junk around. He puts his hands on the outside of the tire and tries to lift it out.

"Like this," I say, and grab the tire by the center. "It isn't just about being strong; it's about putting your body in the right place. It's all about leverage. See?" I say.

155

"Now we need that." I point to the jack, which looks like a toy. "And that." I point to the lug wrench.

"I know," says Eric. "We watched a video in driver's ed. I passed the quiz."

"Well, do it, then," I say. "You know, if somebody stops to help, I might have to kill them. Make sure you put the jack under the frame, solid. Know what I mean?"

Eric kneels down and reaches under the car with his long, spindly arms. I imagine his fingers crawling around in the dark, exploring and finding a place to fit the jack.

"My dad," says Eric. "No car hit him."

"The handle fits in here, like this," I say. "Now, use the weight of your body. The jack will ratchet up each time. You don't have to get it real far off the ground or nothing."

"He just died. It could have happened anywhere. There was a thing wrong in his brain. An aneurysm. It would have happened no matter what he was doing at that moment. He could have been sleeping."

One of the lug nuts is stubborn, or maybe it's just that Eric's boneless hands are weak. "Use the weight of your body," I say again.

"There was nothing anybody could have done. That's what they said after the autopsy. Even if we had been right there with him, we couldn't have helped."

"OK, now put that spare on. Suck it up, you aren't even bleeding."

"There is no way anybody could have saved him."

"Where are the nuts? If you're one short, it's no big deal. They don't have to be super tight . . . not like *you* could make that happen. OK. Release the jack."

"Sometimes people just die."

"Sounds to me like the black helicopters killed him, your dad. Toss the tire in the back. Let's go."

"What?"

"Let's go. You know how to pick up a tire now, do it."

"Not that. The black helicopters. What did you say about the black helicopters?"

"Those People probably killed your dad. That's the way Those People work. He was just trying to change his tire, but they saw him there out in the open and all alone. So they killed him. That's the way Those People work."

That's when the lug wrench hits me.

# One Hour Ago

DISPATCHER: This is 911. What is your emergency?

CALLER: Hello?

DISPATCHER: Hi, what's going on?

CALLER: Please hurry, OK? I'm at a gas station. Listen to me. We need help.

DISPATCHER: We are going to get you some help. All right? We are going to get you some help. I promise. Where are you calling from?

CALLER: It's the pay phone outside a Loaf'n'Jug on the interstate. Please, just listen. I want to tell you where she is.

DISPATCHER: I'm listening. We're going to get you help, OK? And what is your name?

CALLER: My name is Eric. Eric Wade. (LONG PAUSE)

CALLER: Hey, can I just tell you everything and go get my brother? I need to go get him.

DISPATCHER: What is your phone number?

CALLER: You mean the phone number here? At the gas station? Or the phone at home? Can you call my mom? Please, call my mom. Tell her I'm gonna get Corbin. Tell her he's OK. Tell her I'm sorry. He's OK. He's OK. (PAUSE) My phone that I'm on is a pay phone. I'll be at my house, too. I'll give you that number.

DISPATCHER: We just need the number where you are now.

CALLER: Hey, I've gotta go. My brother, he's scared right now. I gotta find him and get him home. We gotta go home.

DISPATCHER: Eric, please wait. I need you to stay on the line.

CALLER: . . . (unintelligible) . . .

DISPATCHER: Eric, I'm having trouble hearing you.

CALLER: I'm sorry but . . . my brother. I need to take care of him.

DISPATCHER: Is he with you? Is the person with you hurt?

CALLER: I think it was my only chance . . . (unintelligible)

DISPATCHER: Eric, Eric, we need you to calm down a little . . . Eric, I understand, but you need to calm down a little. You said someone was hurt. Who got hurt? Was it your brother?

CALLER: No, her. She's in the barrow pit. I left her in the barrow pit. I think maybe I killed her. (unintelligible)

DISPATCHER: I don't understand, Eric. Who is she? She's by the highway? Did someone get hit by a car?

CALLER: I hit her with the lug wrench thing after I changed the tire. (LONG PAUSE) It wasn't an accident. I meant to do it. I'm sorry. (unintelligible)

DISPATCHER: Calm down, Eric.

CALLER: It's the girl that's been on the news.

CALLER: (unintelligible)

DISPATCHER: Which girl?

CALLER: With the bomb. It was her. Valley.

CALLER: (unintelligible) I'm freaking out. I'm sorry, I'll stop, all right?

161

DISPATCHER: That's OK, that's OK.

CALLER: I'm sorry, but I think she's dead.
I put a marker near where she is. I used a
shark my brother made. It's mostly blue. I
put it on the fence by where it happened,
just a little way away. I thought maybe it
might be hard to find the place again. Maybe
if she isn't dead you can save her. Please.

DISPATCHER: There is a deputy on his
way. He's on the way, so just hang tight, OK?

CALLER: OK, I will. Will he help me get my
brother? (PAUSE) I can hear a siren. Is that
them? Thank you. Thank you very much.

# Now

I am here. Cold. The air is solid. This is the world so cold that even the snow is dead. This is the world where I am. And it is black dark. I make my eye open, and nothing changes. I am a little frozen eye.

I taste blood. The blood is in the way of my breath. Everything in my stomach pushes out, and it hurts, but it's warm for a moment. And it's a comfort, but then the warmth fades away, dissolving in the air, and all that's left is the smell of blood and acid. And it hurts.

"Got something. It's the girl." A touch, a finger on my throat. "Got a pulse . . . Can't tell."

The clock is winding down: tick, tick, tick. I am the clock and the clock is me.

"ETA on that chopper? Wait on that to move her, copy. Breathing, air passage seems clear."

Light, light, so much light. It hurts. It stabs right through and burns all red. Open or closed, the red clot of light is floating. What does it want from me?

"Pupil is responsive. Are you with me? If you're with me, can you squeeze my hand? Good! That's good. Yeah, stay with me. She's conscious. Scalp wounds, facial fractures, blow to the back of the head, could be a neck injury. Ten-four, copy that. Waiting on the med crew. OK. I'm going for a minute. Coming back with a blanket, OK? Squeeze my hand. Good girl.

"Your name is Valley? We're going to get you warmed up a little. Not long now. We'll get you to the hospital. We'll get you safe. You with me, Valley?"

Pock-a-pock-pock-POCK-A-POCK. The helicopter shark slides through time and the sky. Its eye is a searchlight that stabs me, blinds me, then slices away, and returns sharp as a tooth.

"What we got?"

"She's breathing, responsive. Possible neck injury, so I waited for you. Her name is Valley. You got Code 10 experience?"

"Code 10 trauma? Sure. A bomb? No. We're hoping we can get somebody on the com."

Another touch. A hand on my arm.

"Good. Hello, Valley. We need to move you a little bit. Can you wiggle your fingers? Good girl. Your foot? Can you move your toes? Great. OK. Let's get the collar on and stabilize her neck. Sorry if this hurts. We'll give something for the pain as soon as we can, promise. OK, let's move her to the backboard. On three: One . . . two . . . three! Checking her heart . . . The vest is in the way. What do we know about the vest?"

"The other kid says she told him she couldn't take it off, but there's no timer, he says. I don't know if we can rely on that."

"Check with dispatch. See how long it will take to get someone out here."

"She can't wait. The head trauma . . ."

"Get a line running. Valley? Are you with us, honey? Can you help us?"

"Dispatch says it will be at least thirty minutes to patch somebody through who knows what to do."

"That's too long. Tell them to be ready at the pad. We're bringing her in."

"You sure?"

"We're going to lift you now, Valley. We're going to take you to the hospital. You're almost home, honey."

Where that smoke is rising, that's home. My mother and my father, waiting for me. The stars are only sparks. They float into the sky and disappear. I see the future.

"We're taking care of you."

The blades on the helicopter slice through time and the sky, the circling hands of a clock, time is going faster and faster.

I have to be brave enough to see this, to know this. My bones and muscles are a fist around my lungs and heart. I can wiggle my fingers. I can move my hand.

Tick, tick, tick.

Time to stop.

Time to touch the trigger on its little dead head.

Time to touch the trigger by my heart.